"If you give me home to Northb... between my legs, I swear I'll punch *you."*

A grin stretched across Boone's face. "Nah, home is where we're supposed to go when life hits you hard. It's good you're here."

Not wanting him to know how much impact something so simple could have on her when it came from him, Faith said, "I'd better go."

"It'll be okay, you know," he said.

She nodded. "Sure."

"Trust me," he said. "Yeah, I know. Why should you trust anything I say when I started out making things harder on you, right? When I acted as if you didn't have any business coming back here? Well, trust me, anyway. I'd never lead you astray."

"Too bad," she joked before she even knew she was going to say anything.

His grin let her know he'd liked it. "Well, maybe not *never.*"

For another moment his too-beautiful-to-belong-to-a-man blue eyes delved into hers and then, without warning, he tipped his head to one side and kissed her.

Dear Reader,

If there's steam rising from this book it's a result of the chemistry between Faith Perry and Boone Pratt. I don't know why, but some characters are just hot, hot, hot for each other.

These two don't start out that way, though. Faith wanted out of her small hometown because there wasn't enough culture. But after having found all of that and a husband to go with it, she also discovered that with the good came some bad. Single again and back in Northbridge, she and her dog, Charlie, need the emergency care of a veterinarian. Enter Boone Pratt…

Faith was hardly aware of Boone while they were growing up together. And she had no idea that she was Boone's dream girl. Now the local vet who's a hunk and a half will treat Faith's dog, but not without letting her know he thinks she's a snob.

Then Boone's old crush finds new life and that's when the heat develops. But is Boone enough to keep Faith home in Northbridge?

I hope you're glad for another trip to the small Montana town and that this cowboy gets to you the way he did to me and to Faith.

Always wishing you happy reading,

Victoria Pade

THE DOCTOR
NEXT DOOR

VICTORIA PADE

Silhouette®

SPECIAL EDITION®

Published by Silhouette Books

America's Publisher of Contemporary Romance

SILHOUETTE BOOKS

ISBN-13: 978-0-373-24883-4
ISBN-10: 0-373-24883-0

THE DOCTOR NEXT DOOR

Copyright © 2008 by Victoria Pade

Books by Victoria Pade

VICTORIA PADE

is a native of Colorado, where she continues to live and work. Her passion—besides writing—is chocolate, which she indulges in frequently and in every form. She loves romance novels and romantic movies—the more lighthearted, the better—but she likes a good, juicy mystery now and then, too.

Chapter One

"What do you have all over your face, Charlie? Did you get into something out there?"

Faith Perry didn't expect an answer from her schnauzer as she let her dog in from the backyard, but the silver-gray purebred responded with a whimper anyway.

"Come here, let me see," Faith urged, bending over to take a look.

But what was soaking the animal's beard and had dribbled onto Charlie's chest and front legs wasn't mud or muck from a yard damp from an early April rain. It was blood.

"Oh! Charlie! Did you kill something?"

Charlie whimpered again and looked at Faith with big, beseeching black eyes that finally caused her to register that the mischievous dog might be hurt.

Faith picked up the fifteen-pound pooch she'd owned for about a year, carried her through the kitchen into the living room and sat down with Charlie in her lap.

On closer inspection, Faith could see that the blood was coming from inside Charlie's mouth.

With some worry that she was going to find a dead bird or part of a squirrel inside, Faith grimaced and pried her pet's jaws apart.

There was more blood in Charlie's mouth but there wasn't anything else. Except for a very broken tooth.

"What did you do?" Faith lamented sympathetically.

It was four o'clock on a Sunday afternoon in her small hometown of Northbridge, Montana. Faith had been in town less than twenty-four hours and she had no idea if the local veterinarian—who had been ancient when she'd left Northbridge eleven years ago—was still in practice. Or if there was another vet or if Northbridge might have joined the twenty-first century and gained an animal hospital.

She did know that she had to get her dog to someone, though. Right away.

"You poor baby," she muttered to Charlie, taking her back into the kitchen.

She set the animal gingerly on the tile floor, gave her a loving stroke and said, "Just sit and let me figure this out."

To Faith's surprise, Charlie minded her.

"Oh, you *must* be in bad shape," Faith said of her pet's unusual compliance.

Until the day before, the house had not been Faith's primary residence. It had only been a place for her and her former husband to stay when they were in town. Because of that, it wasn't well-equipped with things like a current telephone directory. Hoping that she had even an outdated one, she hurried to the laundry room off the kitchen.

"Keep your fingers crossed," she said to the companion who had no fingers to cross.

Still, she counted herself lucky to find the mail-order-catalog-sized phone book in a cupboard and she quickly returned to the kitchen to search the two-year-old listings.

"No, no more old Doc Chapman," she said when she couldn't find the old veterinarian's name listed. "Boone Pratt—he's the vet now," she told Charlie. "I knew that. My sister married his brother—and an emergency call about an animal was the reason he wasn't at the wedding. I should have remembered."

But in the time since Faith had left Northbridge

she hadn't put much effort into keeping up with anyone in the small town other than her family. And even when the information had been shared with her recently, she hadn't retained a lot of it. Her life had been too much of a mess lately for her to have grasped much beyond her own problems and immediate family matters.

Her cell phone was on the counter and she used it to dial the number for the veterinarian's office. Maybe someone was on duty this weekend.

No such luck. On the second ring the other end of the line was answered by a recorded female voice.

Office hours were given before an in-case-of-emergency number.

Cursing her own stupidity for not being prepared with pen and paper, Faith repeated the number out loud, over and over again as she ended the call and dialed it.

"Come on, come on, come on," she said impatiently to each unanswered ring. "You're the only vet in town, what am I going to do if you don't pick up—"

"Yo."

Yo?

"Is this Boone Pratt?" Faith asked.

"Yeah. Who's this?"

Faith reminded herself that she was in Northbridge. Things were much more casual here.

"This is Faith Perry—"

"Faith," he repeated, obviously needing no further

explanation. Of course, it *was* Northbridge. They *had* grown up together, been in the same grade all through school. And her cousin Jared *was* marrying his sister, Mara, next Sunday. It wasn't as if she were a complete stranger even though, to Faith's knowledge, she hadn't set eyes on the man since high school graduation.

"I'm sorry to bother you," she continued, "but I just got to town, my dog seems to have broken a tooth and I guess you're the vet."

"No guessing about it. I am. The only one in town."

He'd gone from the laid-back, friendly *yo* to a much more curt tone of voice. But then they'd never been friendly, so maybe this was his version of professionalism.

"How bad's the tooth?" he demanded.

"Bad enough for me to see that it's broken and for there to be blood all over."

"I'll have to meet you at my office. Do you know where that is?"

Because the directory was still open she was able to read out the address that put him just off of Main Street and only a few blocks from Faith's house.

"That's it," the vet cut her off before she got the complete address out. "I'm in the middle of something at my place outside of town so it'll take me about half an hour to get things under control here and drive in. I'll see you there."

Click.

That was it, he'd hung up.

"Well, okay…" Faith muttered to herself, taken aback by the man's abruptness.

But at that moment manners—or the lack of them— was less a concern than getting Charlie taken care of.

Faith arrived at Boone Pratt's office exactly half an hour after calling him. But when she carried Charlie from the car to the door she found it locked. Peering through a plate-glass window, she saw no sign that anyone was inside, so she sat on the wooden bench below the office window to wait with Charlie in her lap.

Fearing she might hurt the dog, Faith had only gingerly washed the blood off of her pet's fur. Charlie wasn't as much of a mess as she'd been when she'd come in from outside but she wasn't altogether clean, either. Faith was embarrassed to bring the animal in with matted hair, but putting Charlie through a bath had seemed cruel.

Faith had changed her own clothes, though. In the circles she had become accustomed to in the last eleven years it would have been unthinkable to be seen in the sweatpants and T-shirt she'd been wearing to unpack her belongings. Even an emergency trip to the vet in Northbridge had compelled her to slip into an ankle-length skirt and a silk blouse.

Her bittersweet-chocolate-colored hair had been taken from its ponytail, too, and, rather than leaving it to fall to her shoulders, she'd swept it back into an impromptu French twist.

Not even on a day at home did she go without makeup, but she had double-checked to be sure there were no mascara smudges beneath her violet-blue eyes. That her thin, straight nose was powdered. That the high cheekbones that had made it seem as if she'd fit into the patrician class in Connecticut were dusted with blush. And she'd added an ever-so-light touch of gloss to lips that could have been cosmetically plumped-up but that she'd let remain naturally not-too-full in a quiet rebellion against the tides.

All in all, her former mother-in-law would still have barely considered her presentable for a visit to the facialist or the hairdresser, both of whom would make improvements, but it was the best Faith could do in a hurry.

On the other hand, when the grimy red truck pulled up to the curb to park next to her BMW, it didn't seem as if anyone who might emerge from it could have any reason to judge.

Probably because she was worried about her dog, that emergence seemed to be in slow-motion and Faith was more aware of details than of the whole that was being unveiled before her as Boone Pratt got out of the truck.

The first thing she noticed were dusty cowboy boots that were obviously unfamiliar with polish or a boot-buffer. They brought with them long legs encased in jeans rubbed nearly white at all the stress points and caked with mud around hems that were partially there, partially ripped into fringe. There was also a denim shirt that was so threadbare it hung almost diaphanously around a lean torso and broad shoulders. The entire ensemble was grimy.

He didn't look any cleaner from the neck up.

Shockingly handsome, but no cleaner.

And I was worried about Charlie being too dirty to be out in public, Faith thought.

"Boone?" she asked, not intending to sound as put-off as she did.

"Faith?" he countered facetiously.

Had he caught her shock at the way he looked? It wouldn't help anything if he had.

"Thank you for coming. I'm sorry to drag you out on a Sunday afternoon," she said, making sure nothing but gratitude echoed in her voice this time.

"Part of the job," he said dismissively.

She stood and he gave her the once-over, making her wonder, again, if she had given herself away, prompting him to get even.

Or maybe he just found her clothes somehow inappropriate. As eyes the blue of a clear, cool mountain lake assessed her down a hawkish nose, the sneer on a mouth that was devastatingly sexy left her with no doubt of his thoughts. He didn't approve of what he saw any more than she had.

Not attempting to conceal his distaste, he walked from the truck to the office with long, confident strides and unlocked the door.

Faith stood aside until she and Charlie were ushered in by a motion that managed to mock her. She was convinced that this man genuinely disliked her. And considering the change in his response on the phone when she'd identified herself, it seemed as if it wasn't only based on her failure to hide that she'd noticed his lack of cleanliness. But if that was the case, she honestly didn't understand why. They had only coexisted in this same small town while growing up; it wasn't as if they'd ever spoken more than ten words to each other. Why did he seem to have so much animosity? But it was there anyway, unmistakably.

Unless it was just that Boone Pratt had a bad disposition, like her grandfather—who had been the town's pastor and was infamously bad-tempered. But a lifetime of the reverend's unlikable personality had given her a basis of comparison and Faith felt as if there was something more personal when it came to Boone Pratt's bad attitude toward her.

"In there," he ordered, pointing a long index finger in the direction of an examining room off the waiting area they'd just entered.

Faith took Charlie into the other room, setting her pet on the countertop that obviously served as an examining table.

Boone Pratt brought up the rear, going around to the inside of the L-shaped space formed by cupboards and counters. As he came into sight again, he ran his big hands through hair that—without the dust that frosted it—was so dark a brown it was almost black.

He needed a haircut—that was what Faith thought of the unruly mane that grazed his shirt collar and waved away from a ruggedly beautiful face with remarkable bone structure. It was a face the photographer who took her former family's annual portraits would have adored. Sharply defined cheek- and jawbones would have put her ex-husband's and her ex-father-in-law's pie-shaped faces to shame.

After this cursory hair-combing, the vet made a show of washing his hands in the sink that occupied the other section of the counter. As Faith cast a glance down at Charlie, she somehow caught sight of Boone Pratt's derriere. Disreputable jeans or not, it was one fine rear.

Fine enough to make Faith swallow hard to keep her composure.

After the vet had done a thorough job of washing his hands, he turned and came to stand directly opposite her and Charlie, dwarfing them both from a stature that must have been a full three inches over six feet.

"Who do we have here?" he asked in a more pleasant tone aimed at his patient as he held out one hand for the animal to sniff.

"This is Charlie," Faith answered.

"Hi, Charlie," Boone Pratt said soothingly and without so much as a glance at Faith. "Got yourself into trouble, did you, boy?"

"He's a her. I mean, Charlie is a girl. I know it doesn't seem like it from the name, but I got her when she was six months old and that was already what she'd been called and since it seemed to suit her because she's not girlie at all, I just kept it."

More information than was necessary, especially since the vet had looked for himself after Faith's initial correction and he hadn't paid any attention to what she'd said after that.

He stroked Charlie's head with one of those large hands, a gesture so gentle and calming the dog actually began to nuzzle him for more.

Still, Faith felt obligated to warn him. "She's been known to bite vets. They have to muzzle her to cut her nails or do anything with her tail end."

"Guess it's lucky that isn't the end we need to work on, isn't it, girl?" he asked Charlie as if Faith were incidental and he and the dog were sharing an inside joke.

Then, still focused on Charlie, he said, "Are you gonna let me take a look in your mouth?"

His voice was so deep and honeyed with persuasion that Faith almost complied herself. As it was, Charlie—who ordinarily barked and howled and snapped and made each visit to a veterinarian an ordeal—made a liar of Faith and repositioned herself to move nearer to Boone as if *he* were her owner.

"Let's see what we have here," he suggested, easing the animal's jaws apart much as Faith had earlier and with Charlie's willing cooperation.

It didn't take more than one glance for him to add, "Yep, that's a broken tooth, all right."

Then he did a survey of the rest of the animal's mouth before letting loose of Charlie's jaws. Only then did he acknowledge that Faith was there. He returned to petting Charlie, who had now completely gone over to the vet's side and was leaning against him as she curled contentedly into the bare—and very muscular—forearms of the man.

"She's broken away most of her upper right molar—that's the largest tooth in a dog's mouth and there isn't enough of it left for me to salvage it. It'll have to be extracted."

"How did she do that?"

"I don't know. She isn't talking," he answered.

"I mean, aren't dogs supposed to have really tough teeth?" she amended, wishing for some of that niceness he seemed to reserve for Charlie.

"They do have really tough teeth," Boone Pratt

confirmed. "But if they get hold of something tougher, their teeth can break just like a human's."

"And then the teeth have to be pulled?"

"Not always. Sometimes they can be saved—the same as with people. But not in this case."

"Can she do without it?"

"She'll adapt."

"What does the extraction involve? I'm not sure I have the stomach for holding her down while you pull her tooth," Faith confessed.

Boone Pratt frowned at her as if she were out of her mind. "I'll have to call in my tech. We'll do a full physical exam to make sure Charlie is otherwise healthy, but I don't see any indications that she isn't—"

"She is healthy. I had her in for her shots about a month ago. And she's too active to be sick."

Again he seemed to ignore her input and continued. "Then Charlie will be anesthetized and I'll do the extraction. There's no way it could be done with you just holding her down."

"She has to be put out?" That seemed extreme.

"I wouldn't do it if I didn't have to. But if you'd prefer a second opinion, you can take her somewhere else. Billings has vets I can recommend."

"I wasn't doubting you. I just don't have any experience with this sort of thing. I've never even thought about dog dentistry and people aren't given general anesthetic to pull a tooth," Faith defended herself.

Boone Pratt said nothing.

Too bad he wasn't as adept with people as he was with animals.

"And you'll do it now?" Faith asked.

She hadn't meant for her gaze to drop to his soiled clothes again when she'd said that. It had been a reflex in response to thinking that while the office was spotless, Boone Pratt was not. And this time it was clear he'd caught the implication.

"Same old Faith," he said under his breath.

Faith had no idea what that meant. But she didn't have any doubt it was insulting.

"Excuse me?"

He shook his head as if *he* couldn't believe *her,* and acted as if he'd never made the remark.

"I was in the middle of saddle-breaking a horse when you called," he said, clearly begrudging her the explanation. "While my assistant preps Charlie I'll run home for a shower. By the time I get back I guarantee I'll be cleaned up. I may even wash my hands again before I get to work. And wear surgical gloves—we do that here in the land of hayseeds, too," he added sarcastically.

"The land of hayseeds?" she repeated.

"Isn't that what you called Northbridge? The reason you couldn't wait to get the hell out? And now here you are, gracing us with your high-and-mighty, nose-in-the-air presence again. Lucky us."

Faith knew her eyes were wide as she stared at him but she couldn't help it. High-and-mighty? Nose-in-the-air? That was what he thought of her?

"Did I say that—*the land of hayseeds?*" she asked.

"You did."

"When?"

"High school."

"High school? You're mad about something I said over a *decade* ago that I don't even remember saying? About Northbridge?"

"Mad? I'm not mad," he said, again as if she were out of her mind. "I couldn't care less about you or anything you've ever said. I was just letting you know that even if this *is* only Northbridge, things are still done just the way they are in the big city. All conditions and instruments will be sterile, every precaution will be taken to avoid contamination and infection."

No matter how much he denied it, he *sounded* mad and Faith wouldn't let it go. "Did I do something to you that I don't remember?"

"No, ma'am, you didn't," he said as if he were proud that she'd never had the opportunity. "Now, either you want me to do this procedure or you don't. What'll it be?"

Faith didn't have any concerns that he would treat Charlie well—he was already cradling the dog in his arms and Charlie was lounging there trustingly. In the best interest of her pet, Faith decided she should just try to ignore Boone Pratt's dislike of her.

"I'd appreciate it if you would do the procedure," she conceded.

He stepped away from the counter. "I'll take good care of Charlie and have my assistant call you when the extraction is over to let you know how it went."

He was dismissing her. So apparently he didn't intend for her to stay in the office during the procedure.

"And then I'll be able to come get her and take her home?" Faith asked.

"She'll need some looking after when she wakes up, so I'd better keep her with me. At least overnight," Boone Pratt decreed.

"I can look after her," Faith said. "I do take care of her the rest of the time."

"Yeah, I'll bet you get *your* hands dirty," he said cuttingly. Then, with the arch of one eyebrow, he said, "It's up to you if you want to deal with post-op."

Faith honestly wasn't afraid of whatever *post-op* entailed. But she also wanted Charlie to have the best care possible and since, afraid or not, she was completely inexperienced at caring for an animal after surgery, it was only logical to assume that the vet who performed the surgery would be better at it than she would.

So, despite the fact that it was likely confirming

his already negative opinion of her, Faith said, "She's probably better off with you."

"Probably," he said snidely.

Then he took her dog and walked out the door that led to whatever was behind the examining room, leaving Faith staring, slack-jawed, at the door he closed behind himself.

"The only thing worse than a hayseed is a rude, nasty hayseed," she muttered to herself.

"I heard that," came Boone Pratt's deep voice from just beyond that door.

Faith wasn't thrilled to know he'd heard her.

But still, loud enough for him to also hear, she said, "Good!"

Then she turned tail and walked out of the office of a man who might be drop-dead gorgeous but who—as far as she was concerned—could just drop dead.

Well, after he fixed Charlie's tooth, anyway.

Chapter Two

"Uh, Miss Charlie, the rule in this house is that the animals stay off the bed—that's why you have a pillow on the floor," Boone Pratt informed the schnauzer early Monday morning when he awoke to his patient sitting beside him on his king-sized mattress, facing him with an unwavering—and pitiful—stare.

His own five dogs—all of them at least four times bigger than the schnauzer—were looking on from various spots around his bedroom, probably wondering at the smaller mutt's audacity.

But reprimanded or not, Charlie curled up against

Boone's side with a small whine to let him know she still didn't feel well.

"I know, nobody likes to be sick," he commiserated, curving one arm around her to pet her with a minimum of effort.

His alarm hadn't yet gone off so he closed his eyes in hopes of catching a little snooze-time. He'd been up most of the night with Charlie. As happened with a lot of animals, the anesthetic had caused vomiting. Plus the particular pain medication he'd administered sometimes had the side-effect of inspiring a vocal response which had left her whimpering on every exhale. He had known she wasn't hurting and it was nothing to be concerned about, but it always upset pet owners. The possibility of those two things happening were why he'd thought it better to keep Charlie with him rather than send her home after extracting her tooth. Especially home with Faith Perry.

As if Charlie knew that Faith had just crossed Boone's mind, the dog nudged against his side in what felt like a criticizing elbow-jab that made him think about Faith and their encounter the day before.

"Yeah, I know, I should have my ass kicked for the way I acted yesterday," he admitted to her dog.

And he didn't even have a good reason for how he'd treated Charlie's mom.

"I'm really not a jerk, you know," he told Charlie. But what he didn't confide—even to the animal—

was what had been behind his behavior. It was something he'd never told anyone. Ever. Something that made him flinch just remembering it.

The first crush he'd had on a girl had been on Faith Perry.

And he could hardly stand thinking about it.

It hadn't been some macho, I'm-the-man kind of crush. If it had, it wouldn't have been such a big deal. But he hadn't been an I'm-the-man kind of kid.

He'd had bad skin and braces on his teeth. He'd been barely five and a half feet tall, stocky, backward, awkward and immature at seventeen when—from out of nowhere—the late bloomer who had spent more time with animals than people had discovered he couldn't think about anything but Faith Perry.

And the crush itself? That had been a doe-eyed, tongue-tied, trip-over-his-own-feet, blushing, can't-control-his-body's-reaction crush. The kind of crush that he would have been ridiculed for if anyone had known. The kind that was completely hopeless and had just made him feel all the more inadequate.

Especially because it had been on someone who was almost unaware that he was alive and had never made a secret of the fact that she couldn't wait to get out of this one-horse town and away from everything and everyone in it to have a cultured life with classier people. Blue bloods, that's what she'd aspired to, hobknobbing with blue bloods.

And every time he'd gotten anywhere near her, every time he'd picked up a book or a pencil she'd dropped, offered her notes from a class she'd missed or any of the other million things he'd done just to be near her, she'd looked at him the way she had when he'd first faced her in front of his office yesterday—as though he were the prime example of the backwater hicks she'd wanted to rise above.

So he'd slumped his way through those last two years of high school feeling rejected and resentful and inept.

As much as he'd worshipped her, he'd hated her.

And yesterday he'd punished her for it.

Okay, maybe I am a jerk....

On the other hand, he also didn't think much of people who believed they were better than others and, particularly, people who believed they were too good for his hometown and the lifestyle and the values that went with it.

But that still didn't excuse his behavior.

It wasn't how he'd planned to act in anticipation of making contact with her again.

He didn't know why, but just the thought of Faith Perry had made him uncomfortable since his crush had died a natural death years and years ago. He supposed she reminded him of something he'd rather forget: a miserable, agony-filled adolescent phase he wished he'd never gone through. A phase that embarrassed him now even if he *had* managed to avoid embarrassing himself—on the whole—back then. So, since she'd left, whenever he'd heard through the grapevine that Faith was coming to town to visit family, he'd avoided places where he might run into her.

The problem recently, though, had become weddings.

Earlier this year there was the wedding of his brother, Cam, and her sister, Eden. Now it was her cousin Jared, marrying his sister, Mara.

For Cam's and Eden's wedding Faith only came to town for the day. He'd known that totally avoiding her was not going to be possible, but he'd planned to keep his distance. To stay across any room they were in together. To observe nothing but scant courtesies and go his own way.

Then he'd ended up being called to an emergency surgery that had kept him from attending the entire event. Problem solved.

For Mara's wedding he'd figured he'd just activate that former plan—avoidance and distance.

But then he'd answered his cell phone yesterday and she'd been on the other end of the line and it had set something off in him from that long-ago silent humiliation.

He'd tried to pull in the reins on it and he'd thought he'd done a pretty good job until he'd stepped out of his truck and watched her majesty recoil at that first look at him.

That's right, he'd wanted to say to her, *I'm covered in dirt and I'm still a hayseed in the land of hayseeds you didn't want any part of.*

And she was still Miss Priss, sitting there on his bench all stiff and prim and proper, her hair and her clothes making her look like some stereotype of a spinster librarian.

Not that she hadn't looked good. Faith the woman was even better-looking than Faith the girl had been, and he'd thought she was the prettiest girl in town then. Now she was full-out, hands-down beautiful.

Even trussed-up, her hair had glistened in the sunlight. It was the burnished sienna color of the mole sauce he ate on enchiladas.

Her face hadn't aged, it had grown refined and delicate, with skin as smooth and pale and flawless as the cream that rose to the top of fresh milk.

Her mouth just had to taste sweet—that was what he'd thought before he'd left his truck, when he'd had his first glimpse of her. It curved up at the corners and dipped low in the center to form a sort of languid heart shape that was the shade of pale pink rosebuds.

And before she'd skewered him with that repulsed glare, he'd thought that even the color of her eyes was more intense—some combination of purple and blue— though still as sparkling as morning dew in the meadow.

He'd steeled himself before getting out of the truck, worrying that one look from those eyes might make him stumble or fall just the way it would have done when he was seventeen. But then she'd helped him avoid that with the instant revulsion he'd seen on her face and it had been like a bucket of cold water dumped over his head.

Yeah, sure, she'd covered it up in a hurry. She'd apologized for bringing him in on his day off, for bothering him. She'd thanked him for coming and hadn't treated him like a lowlife. But by then it was too late. He'd known what she was thinking even before she'd made it to her feet. And he just hadn't been able to be nice.

Of course he *had* been able to notice the rest of her when she'd stood. To register that there was nothing bad about the body, either. At least as far as he could tell through those shapeless clothes she'd had on. There was a little sway to hips that were just the right width as she'd gone into the office ahead of him, and enough behind the buttons of that boring blouse Charlie was snuggled up to on the countertop to let it be known she wasn't flat-chested—to make him wonder if he should have untucked his shirt before he'd left home.

But despite how she looked, despite her cover-up courtesy, he'd still been on his worst behavior.

So I proved I can be as big a clod as she thinks I am....

Actually, what was it she'd said when she'd thought he was out of earshot? That the only thing worse than a hayseed was a rude, nasty hayseed.

Miss Priss could bark back after all.

That had to go against the dictates of her highfalutin ways now, didn't it?

But even though she'd been insulting him, it made him smile to think that he'd gotten a rise out of her.

Still, the way things had gone the day before were not how he wanted things to be at his sister's wedding. Mara didn't deserve that. Hell, if push came to shove, he had to admit that Faith Perry didn't deserve it, either. She'd never actually done anything to him. So what if he—and the rest of Northbridge—didn't live up to her standards? That was her problem. Her loss.

But when it came to him and who he was, he didn't want to be a jerk. Not even to someone who thought she was better than he was.

In fact, he might go so far as to prove he was the bigger person and apologize for the way he'd treated her.

"What would your mom think of that, Charlie?" he asked the pooch at his side. Then he answered his own question, "She'd probably just think she had it coming, huh?"

Charlie sighed and nuzzled his hand to make him pet her once more. Boone did, wondering if the dog spent every night sleeping with Faith. Right beside her in bed where her hair would be free and so would her body under some filmy little nightgown....

Jealousy? Was he actually feeling even a tiny pinch envious of a dog?

Oh, no, uh-uh, he told himself.

She might be beautiful, but she wasn't getting to him. Not a chance in hell. He'd never set himself up for *that* now. No way.

Not when he'd been so vividly reminded yesterday that it was only blue blood that impressed her.

And his was as red as it came.

"Do we have a verdict yet?"

Faith had stopped by her sister Eden's house late Monday afternoon on her way to the vet's office. It was such a beautiful spring day that Eden was sitting outside on her front porch steps when Faith arrived. Faith had an ulterior motive for the visit but was in no hurry, so she'd accepted her sister's invitation to join her.

"A verdict?" Faith asked in response to Eden's question after she'd perched beside her sister on the top porch step. "About what?"

"Northbridge—if you're staying forever or for a while, or if you're already thinking about leaving as soon as cousin Jared's wedding is over."

"I just got here Saturday night," Faith reminded.

"And did you bring your whole wardrobe or only enough for a quick trip?"

Faith knew what her sister was getting at. "I brought enough for a while but not everything I own. The rest is still at the apartment in New Haven that Shu bought as part of the divorce settlement—"

"So you're keeping the apartment?"

"I don't know yet."

"Then there's the chance that you'll actually live there?"

Faith heard her sister's disappointment. Now that Eden had moved back to Northbridge and married a local cop—Boone Pratt's brother, Cam—Eden and their other sister, Eve, who also lived in Northbridge, were hoping that Faith would make her home in the small town, too. They'd been trying to persuade Faith for months now and Faith knew Eden was fishing for a sign she had made her decision. But Faith hadn't and so couldn't give Eden the answer she was looking for. Or any answer at all, really.

"I still don't know what I'm going to do," Faith said. "There *is* the apartment in Connecticut and I have an offer to go back to work full-time there if I want to—"

"With the same party and event planners you were working for when you met Shu—isn't that what Eve said?"

"Yes. The Fosters wouldn't hear of me working

when I was married. That wasn't my role as Shu's wife. But I just had some dealings with my old cohorts over the plans for the opening of Nedra's gallery and they said there was a spot for me if I wanted a job." Nedra was Nedra Carpenter, an old college friend of Faith's whom Eden had met several times during her visits to Connecticut.

"But you don't *have* to work," Eden reminded.

Faith shrugged. "No, I don't *have* to. The settlement was beefed up substantially to keep me quiet. But I also don't know what I'll do with myself it I don't work. That's the problem—I don't know what I want any more than I know what I'm going to do. I'm hoping to sort through it all here, remember? It was your idea when I visited in January for me to come back, bask in the peace and quiet and see if I could get my bearings again."

Faith had come to Northbridge at the start of the year for just a day to Eden's wedding to briefly touch base with her family when they were in turmoil over the revelation that the grandmother they'd all believed to have run off with a bank robber more than forty years ago had secretly returned to work as a clerk at the dry cleaners. Because Faith had been packing up and leaving her in-laws' house, one day was all she'd been able to spare. But Eden and Eve had persuaded her to spend some time in Northbridge to regroup once the last loose ends of her divorce were tied up. And the upcoming wedding was the perfect time to do just that.

"And you haven't come any closer to getting those bearings between January and now?" Eden asked.

Faith shrugged again. "It isn't easy when I find myself questioning everything I've been so sure of my whole life. You had the rug pulled out from under you when Alika was killed in the line of duty in Hawaii, you had trouble being able to accept that Cam was a cop, too, and in similar kinds of danger on the job—"

"That almost seems silly now that I've really settled into Northbridge. Sometimes I wonder why we even need cops around here."

"Still, as bad as it was to lose Alika, and as hard as it was to get over your fear so you could be with Cam, you never had to doubt your choice of Alika as a husband or doubt the life you two had together. You didn't have to look back and see that what you thought was real wasn't and ask yourself if you were blind or stupid or if you'd gone after the wrong thing in the first place. Alika's death left you afraid of being with another cop, not wondering if you were an idiot who couldn't see what was right in front of your face for years. But me... I have to wonder if, somehow, I asked for what I got."

"Oh, Faith, how could you have asked for what you got?"

Faith shrugged a third time. "I got what I asked for and the rest came with it."

"But what came with it was not what anyone would have asked for or could have expected."

"Maybe not—"

"No maybe about it."

"The bottom line, Eden, is that on the surface I got exactly what I wanted. What I'd always wanted. And it turned out so badly that now… Now I just don't know."

"So you can stay here and figure it out," Eden concluded.

"Or I can stay here *until* I figure it out," Faith said, not wanting to commit to more than that when it came to Northbridge.

It seemed like a good time to change the subject so she opted to embark on her ulterior motive. "What are you up to for the next hour or so?" she asked her sister.

Eden held up a cell phone. "I'm waiting for a call to tell me whether the last fairy sketches are all right."

Eden had ended her career as a forensic artist and was now illustrating a children's book.

"You could take your phone with you and help me out," Faith proposed hopefully.

"Help you out with what?"

"Your brother-in-law. According to his receptionist, he's keeping Charlie another night. I guess Charlie still isn't eating or drinking and he needs to watch her. But I wanted to at least visit her. The receptionist put me on hold to ask if that would be all right. He okayed it but the receptionist said his schedule today was full, so would I come after the last appointment. As if my being at the office would interfere with anything."

Eden either didn't notice the derisive note in Faith's voice or she chose not to mention it. Instead she said, "What does that have to do with me?"

"I don't particularly want to go alone. Your brother-in-law is a creep."

"Boone?" Eden said with a laugh. "You have to be kidding. Boone's a pussycat."

"He is not. He's rude and obnoxious and we sort of had a fight yesterday. I was hoping I could pick up Charlie this morning and not even *see* him, but now not only don't I get to take Charlie home, I'm sure I'll have to see bad-news Boone while I'm visiting my dog."

"Are you sure we're talking about the same person? The tall, hunky guy who resembles my husband except he has longer, darker hair and lighter eyes and when he smiles he gets those creases down his cheeks?"

"I wouldn't know what happens when he smiles because I didn't see anything that came close to a smile. But yes, longer, darker hair—at least I think it's darker underneath the layer of dirt that was covering him from head to toe."

"Dirt?"

"He said something about coming straight from saddlebreaking a horse."

"That would probably get him pretty dirty."

"But he's in the medical profession. No medical professional should—"

"Didn't you have to call him in on his day off? In an emergency? Seems to me you take what you get under those conditions."

"Still. He didn't even apologize for it or explain it until late in the game. And dirty or not, he was awful."

"To Charlie?"

"No, he was fine to Charlie. He was awful to me."

"Seriously?"

"Why would I make this up?" Faith asked. "He called me high-and-mighty and nose-in-the-air. He brought up something I guess I said in high school about Northbridge being the land of the hayseeds and then he said some weird stuff about how he couldn't care less about me or about anything to do with me."

"Boone?" Eden repeated with more disbelief.

"I asked him if I'd done something to make him mad. He said no—that was the part about how he couldn't care less—but he *acted* mad. He acted as if he hated me."

"Why would he hate you?"

"Good question. As far as I know, I haven't seen

him since high school. Not even when I've come to Northbridge to visit. Have I turned into some snooty bitch who goes around offending people without realizing it?"

"*You*, a snooty bitch?" Eden repeated with a laugh at how ridiculous that sounded. "You're the one who was in trouble with your mother-in-law for not being snooty enough. Didn't you get your wrists slapped for buying birthday and Christmas gifts for the house staff, and letting them call you by your first name? But Boone? Honestly, since coming back to Northbridge and hanging around with the Pratt family I've never seen him be anything but nice and even-tempered and calm. I've certainly never seen him be a creep. It just doesn't sound like Boone."

"Well, unless he has an evil twin, it *was* Boone."

"Did you do something to him when we were kids?"

"I thought about it all night and most of today, but I can't think of anything. I mean, I remember him being short and kind of pudgy. I remember that he almost never talked and I think sometimes he had wildlife in his pockets—"

Eden laughed. "Wildlife?"

"Like frogs or toads or turtles or lizardy things— the kind of things little boys might have in their pockets—but we were in high school. I remember him always turning red, too. As if he was embarrassed even when there wasn't anything to be embarrassed about.

But I never made fun of him or anything. I never really had much to do with him beyond sitting in front of him in classes where seating was alphabetical."

"Maybe that's what rubbed him wrong—that you *didn't* have anything to do with him," Eden suggested.

"That I didn't say hi to him in homeroom over a decade ago?"

"That does seem far-fetched."

"So what's up with him?"

Eden shrugged this time. "I couldn't tell you."

"So will you go with me to visit Charlie and save me from more of his bad attitude?"

"I really can't, Faith. This call is important and Cam should be home any minute and we need to—"

"You're just going to throw me to the wolf?"

"Give him another chance. Maybe he had a bad day yesterday and he'll be nice today."

"That would be an even bigger change than the change in his looks," Faith said as she stood to leave, wishing all the while she was saying goodbye to her sister that Boone Pratt's looks *hadn't* changed.

Because maybe if they hadn't she might have been able to stop thinking about the way he looked.

Which was something she hadn't quite managed. Over the past twenty-four hours the image of him had stayed in her mind's eye no matter what she'd done to switch channels.

* * *

When Faith arrived at the veterinarian's office, Boone Pratt's truck and another car were parked in front of the building, which was shaded by a semi-circle of tall pine trees. She had no idea if the other car belonged to a pet owner or to one of Boone Pratt's employees. Not wanting to set him off by going inside if he was still involved in his last appointment, she waited until a woman came out and got into the other car. Only then did Faith leave her own vehicle, not appreciating how on-edge she felt at the prospect of having to go through an ogre to get to her pet.

Inside, the office was quiet. Boone Pratt must have heard the door open and close because from some-where in back came his deep voice. "Is that you, Faith?"

That didn't sound ogreish. Or as abrasive as the previous day. But not even a more amiable tone made her feel any better as she answered. "Yes, it's me."

"We'll be right out."

Was there going to be some courtesy today? That *was* a change.

Faith sat on the cushioned bench seat built into the wall across from the receptionist's station. She flicked a piece of lint off the skirt that was very much like the ankle-length A-line she'd worn the day before except that it was brown. On top she had on another blouse—

this one also white but with a tan fleck that distinguished it from what she'd worn on Sunday.

Her hair was tied at her nape with a scarf and while she'd felt overdressed when she'd been sitting on her sister's step—with Eden in jeans and a T-shirt—she didn't think she was overdressed now.

At least she didn't until Boone Pratt brought Charlie out into the waiting area.

Boone was clean today. Perfectly. His dark wavy hair, his extravagantly handsome face, his hands and nails, even his cowboy boots showed not a speck of the dust of the day before. His clothes were spotless, too, but beneath the long white lab coat that gave him a professional air were jeans and a chambray shirt. And it occurred to Faith only then that maybe she should find some more casual attire for Northbridge.

But her dog was following behind him as he joined her and she turned her focus there.

"Oh, my poor baby! Are you sick?" she asked the dog without greeting Boone Pratt.

Charlie wagged her tail, obviously happy to see Faith.

"She's feeling pretty sorry for herself," Boone said as Faith scooped up her pet to hold in her lap.

A section of Charlie's front paw was shaved but other than that she, too, was cleaner than she had been the previous day and she smelled like she'd been given a bath.

"We just got her to eat a little food and take a few laps of water," Boone Pratt was saying despite the fact that Faith had yet to address him and was looking only at her schnauzer. "If she can finally hold that down and maybe take in a little more later tonight she can go home tomorrow."

"What made her so sick?" Faith asked, still not taking her eyes off of Charlie.

"Some dogs just don't tolerate the anesthetic or the pain medication as well as others. There's nothing to worry about. She had enough pep this afternoon to hop onto my desk chair. Then she barked like crazy at the cat that was in here half an hour ago, so she's really fine. She just needs to get up to speed again and I think she'll be there tomorrow. The extraction went well and there's no infection. When her appetite comes back and she's rehydrated she'll be good as new."

Boone Pratt moved from where he'd been standing in front of Faith.

Feeling as if the coast was clear, Faith glanced up from Charlie to see what Boone was doing.

He was behind the reception counter removing his lab coat, rolling it up and tossing it somewhere Faith couldn't see.

Then he returned to the waiting area.

Faith looked down at Charlie once more but out of the corner of her eye she saw Boone lean against the wall. He folded his arms across his chest, placed one ankle over the other and seemed to settle in to watch her.

It was unnerving and, under other circumstances, with someone else, Faith would have made conversation to ease the tension. But she wasn't feeling friendly and was trying to avoid saying the wrong thing. So she pretended to be aware of only Charlie. When, in fact, she was much, much more aware of Boone Pratt than she wished to be. Aware and not unaffected by the sight of the man all cleaned up.

"I owe you an apology for yesterday," he said suddenly. "That's why I asked that you not come in until after office hours. You were right, I was rude and nasty to you."

He'd overheard the parting shot.

But recalling that she *had* said that and that Eden thought better of him than she did, Faith decided to give him the benefit of the doubt and take a step of her own in the direction of peace.

Still without raising her eyes, she seized on the assumption that he'd been peeved because of something she'd done unknowingly and she said, "If I snubbed you one of the times I've been in town since high school it wasn't intentional. You weren't at Eden's wedding and I only knew you were you yesterday because… Well, because it was you who was meeting me here. You don't look like the same person you did all those years ago. I would never have recognized you if we did just run into each other on the street."

"Yeah, I had quite a growth spurt first year of college. But yesterday was just some old stuff of my own, it wasn't that you'd snubbed me sometime in the last eleven years."

"I did something to you when we were kids?" she asked, believing that that was what his *old stuff* stemmed from.

"It's not like that, no. I guess I just took offense at how much you hated Northbridge and those of us in it—"

"Hate is a little strong. I just wanted something different. There was nothing personal in it."

"I'm sure there wasn't. And hey, so we aren't your cup of tea, that's just the way it is. But yesterday, re-membering it, set me off. Anyway, like I said, I apologize. It was uncalled for and out of line and Charlie here let me know it in no uncertain terms."

That made Faith smile and look up from her dog to see that Boone Pratt was smiling slightly, too. And that yes, when he did, his remarkable face formed deep creases in his cheeks that only added to how great-looking he was.

"Charlie let you know in no uncertain terms?" she repeated. "Charlie talked to you?"

"You mean she *doesn't* talk to you?" he joked.

"She *is* good at letting me know what she wants," Faith conceded.

"Well, she let me know that she didn't approve of how I treated her mom yesterday and I agreed she was right. So maybe we can start over?"

"Okay," Faith said, a bit leery but again recalling that Eden liked him.

In the interest of starting over, Faith finally opted for friendliness. As Charlie curled up in her lap, she said, "Did you know that I've been enlisted to organize a fund-raiser for a horse rescue? And in a hurry—apparently the mayor wants it to happen next Saturday in conjunction with some sort of auction?"

She ended that with a question because she knew next to nothing about the project.

"A horse auction," he said. "The horse rescue is my baby. I'm doing the auction. I knew the mayor was going to try to whip up something to go along with it, but this is the first I've heard of your being in on it. How'd that happen? Didn't you just get to town?"

"I was enlisted by phone through my sisters. If I had to guess, I'd say Eve and Eden probably volunteered me. They're saying that the mayor heard I would be back in Northbridge, somehow knew about my experience as an event planner and thought I was just the person for the job, but that seems fishy to me."

"You think they offered you up for it?"

"My sisters want me to move back permanently—that's part of what I'm supposed to be here thinking over. I'm sure they figured this would get me involved in the community again, that it would help convince me to stay. But however it happened, I said I'd do it. Even though it will be a huge crunch to pull it off on such short notice."

Faith had the impression that Boone wasn't particularly happy to hear that she was on board, but he was trying not to show it.

Then, with some leeriness of his own, he said, "Do you have any idea yet what you'll do?"

"Actually it was a long drive here from Connecticut and I had a lot of time to think, so yes, I do. I was thinking that it's spring and that's a big time for people to clean out closets and basements and garages and cellars and attics. So I thought why not have them donate what they want to get rid of and arrange a flea market in the town square with all the proceeds to go to the horse rescue."

She didn't have a clue as to why he looked so surprised, but he did.

"Bad idea?" she assumed to explain it.

"No, that's a good idea. A terrific one, in fact."

"But you *expected* me to come up with a bad idea?" she asked, still confused by the shocked expression she'd prompted.

He smiled again, sheepishly this time, and she had to admit it was appealing. Very appealing.

"When you said you were enlisted to do the fund-raiser I had a flash of a black-tie affair that not many people would come out for. But a flea market? That's perfect for Northbridge. The whole town will get into that."

"I'm glad you like it."

"It'll also bring out more folks for the auction, maybe increase the odds of selling some of the horses so I can get them off my hands."

"Do you keep some of the rescued horses yourself?"

"More than I should. The same goes for a couple of other ranches around here. That's why we need to do the auction and why the mayor said he'd do what he could to raise some money for us—funds are down after caring for as many animals as we have in the last month or so."

"I didn't think there were that many horses rescued at any given time."

"It varies."

"Has there been a big influx lately?"

"We had a hard winter. Closer to the big cities they see more neglect, abuse, problems from overcrowding, abandonment, that sort of thing. We can run into that here, too, but in the open countryside we're more likely to see wild horses that have been hurt or stranded. Or, like now, a lot that couldn't find food through the winter and were dying of starvation. That's why we're overcrowded right now."

"You've been feeding them?"

"Feeding them, nursing them back to health. But we can't just keep them all. Eventually, when the horses are ready, something has to be done with them. So we hold periodic auctions."

"To make way for more horses that need help."

"Right."

So he had dimples and he did good deeds even beyond the call of duty that had brought him to Charlie's rescue yesterday. Faith was beginning to see why her sister had been shocked by her complaints about him.

And since that left Faith wondering again about what part she might have played—however unwittingly—in the previous day's events, she wanted to make sure she was particularly conscientious today. Which seemed to mean not dragging out her visit to Charlie.

"I'm sure you've put in a full day and want to get home," she said then. "Your receptionist said you're keeping Charlie there with you?"

"I have five dogs so one more doesn't make much difference."

"And Charlie is doing all right with the other dogs?" It was Faith's turn to be shocked.

"Sure," he said as if he didn't understand the question.

Faith decided against telling him that Charlie was usually horrible around anyone else's pets.

Instead, she said, "And you think I'll be able to take her home tomorrow?"

"I'd plan on it."

"Good. My house is pretty empty without her," Faith said, standing and handing her schnauzer back to Boone.

Charlie had no qualms about being returned to the vet—another surprise—and actually tipped her head back once she was in his arms, lovingly licking the underside of Boone's chin.

"Yes, you're a good girl," Boone cooed to her, placing a light kiss to the top of Charlie's head.

And Faith felt a pang.

She wasn't sure of what, but it came in response to that kiss.

It must have been over seeing how much her dog liked Boone, she decided. Ordinarily Charlie's loyalty to her was intense and Charlie didn't warm up to anyone else, so Faith wasn't accustomed to sharing her affections.

"I'll call in the morning," she said as she made her way to the door with Boone and Charlie bringing up the rear.

"Okay," the vet said. "And don't worry, I know

Charlie isn't being herself but she'll be back to normal soon."

Faith nodded, partially turning to give her dog one last pet and kiss the top of Charlie's head herself before saying goodbye.

"Have a nice night," Boone called as she went out.

"You, too," she responded with one last glance at man and dog.

And one last pang.

And while it still seemed logical that the pang was from leaving Charlie with someone else, it almost felt as if that wasn't exactly the cause.

It almost felt as if that pang was jealousy.

Jealousy of her pet.

Who was in Boone Pratt's arms.

But *that* couldn't possibly be the case, she told herself.

And yet, the pang was there and with it was some curiosity about what it might feel like to have Boone Pratt's big hands stroking her....

Chapter Three

When Faith's doorbell rang at seven-thirty Tuesday night there were two possibilities for who could be on her front porch.

The first was that it was the delivery person from the Chinese restaurant, Northbridge's newest addition.

The second possibility was that it was Boone Pratt.

And even though she was starving, she was secretly—and curiously—rooting for the Boone possibility.

As she reached for the handle she heard Charlie's demanding let-me-in yip to give her advance warning of who had rung the bell.

An inexplicable smile sprang to her lips and she instantly suppressed it. Boone Pratt didn't need to know that after not being able to stop thinking about him since leaving his office on Sunday evening, she was so happy for the chance to see him again that she was nearly giddy. So she made sure she was composed and showing no signs of her delight by the time she opened the door.

"Dog delivery," Boone announced in greeting.

"It had to be that or Chinese food," Faith said, stepping out of the way as Charlie charged inside.

"She's better," Faith observed, surprised by the improvement in her pet. "And not even on a leash."

"She's fine," Boone assured.

"Come in," Faith invited.

It was not as spontaneous an invitation as she made it sound.

Before she'd had the chance to call Boone's office that morning to ask when she could pick up Charlie, Boone's receptionist had phoned to tell her Charlie was with Boone and that Boone had gone from home to an emergency on a farm far outside of Northbridge. The receptionist had said she would let Faith know when he got to the office.

Then the receptionist had called later to say the emergency was going to occupy Boone all day and that—if it was all right with Faith—he would bring Charlie by her house later this evening.

So Faith had known for hours that Boone would be coming by tonight and she'd given the whole prospect a great deal of thought. Beginning with just how friendly she should be when she was with him again.

She'd been surprised with how friendly she wanted to be, surprised how much the idea of his coming over had pleased her. She'd spent the better part of the afternoon deliberating about what to wear, how to do her hair, how to act, whether or not to ask him in, what to say if she did and how to say it. She'd even caught herself practicing in the mirror when she'd only intended to pluck her eyebrows.

And despite telling herself that there was no reason for her to be doing or thinking any of what she'd done or thought, in the end she'd hated the idea of Boone merely dropping off Charlie and leaving. And then she'd told herself that asking him in when he was personally bringing her dog home was nothing more than hometown hospitality.

Hometown hospitality that included deep-conditioning her hair and wearing it loose around her shoulders, paying special attention to her blush and mascara, ironing perfect creases into her khaki slacks and changing tops seven times before she'd settled on the pale yellow sweater set she had on.

She'd told herself it was nothing more than hometown hospitality that prompted her to wait to order her dinner until Boone's promised call, telling her he was on his way. And to order at least three times more food than she would have ordered for herself.

Her rehearsed invitation for him to come in must have seemed as innocent as she'd intended it to, though, because Boone merely accepted it by stepping inside.

"I don't know what she was like before, but I'm betting she's her old self," he said as he did.

Charlie, he's talking about Charlie, Faith had to remind herself, realizing only then that telling her about her dog's health was likely *why* Boone had accepted her invitation. That it was purely business. As it should have been. She was simply showing him hometown hospitality and he was simply showing her the courtesy he probably offered every pet owner. That's all there was to it, that's all there *should* have been to it. It had nothing to do with attraction of any kind....

"Come in and sit," she invited, leading him from the door that opened into the living room to the black leather sofa and the matching white leather chair that Charlie had already jumped up on.

"Charlie, you know you aren't supposed to be on that chair," she said when she spotted her schnauzer sitting proudly in the middle of it. "Please get down."

Charlie glanced up at her but didn't budge. As usual.

"Charlie, down," Boone said from behind Faith.

Charlie hopped down.

"She listened to you," Faith said in amazement.

Boone sat in the chair Charlie had vacated but made no comment before outlining the progression of her dog's health in the last twenty-four hours.

Faith wondered if she was a terrible pet owner, but she was only half listening as she took in the sight of Boone.

For someone who had been attending to a farm-animal emergency, he looked remarkably good. He had on semidark blue jeans, a completely unwrinkled crisp white dress shirt with the sleeves rolled to his elbows and buffed and polished cowboy boots. Plus his longish hair was clean, his dauntingly handsome face was freshly shaven and he smelled like spring rain—a cologne she wasn't familiar with but liked more than she wished she did.

Had he gone home to shower and shave before bringing Charlie? she wondered suddenly.

If he had it was more likely because whatever had kept him busy today had left him in need, that it had nothing to do with her. She told herself this to keep from feeling unduly flattered. Just because she had found thoughts of him impossible to shake didn't mean he'd had the same problem with thoughts of her. Why would he have?

"…no dry food—canned food only—for the next week to give her mouth a chance to heal. Nothing but soft treats, too. But other than that, she's perfectly healthy and full of personality," Boone was saying when Faith realized he was wrapping up his account of Charlie and that she'd better pay attention.

The doorbell rang again just then and Charlie leaped into action just as she always did—running for the door, barking so loudly it was jarring.

"You're expecting company—that's why you're dressed up again," Boone said.

He *still* thought she'd overdone it? And she hadn't even worn the pearls that usually went with the sweater set...

"I'll take off," Boone added over the ruckus.

"No!"

Faith regretted the urgency in her voice and hoped the noise her dog was making camouflaged it. Then, forcing nonchalance again, she said, "That's just dinner. Remember? I told you I'd ordered Chinese food."

Charlie continued to bark and Faith raised her voice to beg the dog to stop.

As with the chair, Charlie ignored her and continued the rant at the door.

"Charlie, no. Come," Boone said, not raising his voice at all.

To Faith's amazement, the dog stopped and instantly rejoined them in the living room.

Where Boone stood. "I should go and let you eat," he said.

"There's a ton of food," Faith countered in a hurry,

standing, too. "Since it's my first time I wanted to try a little of a lot of things. Then I'll know from here on what's good and what isn't. If you haven't eaten, you could stay...."

The second invitation she'd rehearsed. Had it sounded unplanned? Or had she just given herself away?

Hoping to cover her tracks if she had, she made up a reason and added, "Maybe you can tell me what kind of spell you've put on my dog to get her to behave."

"You seriously want me to have dinner with you?" Boone asked, once again not addressing her astonishment over his control of her dog but showing some of his own astonishment at her suggestion.

"Seriously," Faith confirmed. "Unless you have plans..." Which could have been why he'd come looking—and smelling—as good as he did.

"I was just going to pick up something to eat on my way home."

"So you might as well stay," Faith said, feeling an inordinate amount of satisfaction to learn that he hadn't intended to see anyone but her tonight.

"You're sure?" he asked as if this might be a trap.

"I'm sure," she confirmed, wishing he didn't still seem so wary of her as she went to answer the door.

Charlie didn't run along beside her and try to rush out the minute she opened it. That came as another surprise. As she accepted several bags of food she looked back to see the schnauzer calmly sitting at Boone's feet.

"We could eat on the coffee table," Faith said when she turned back to Boone, "but we won't have any peace from Charlie. She'll have her nose in everything and she'll steal whatever she can reach. So we're probably better off in the kitchen. Just don't ever leave your chair not pushed in or she'll jump up there, too, and help herself."

"Really...." Boone said, following her as Faith went around the half wall that was the only separation between living room and kitchen.

"There's no dining room," Faith continued, feeling the need to outline her humble surroundings for no reason she understood. "The whole place doesn't amount to much," she said as she unloaded the sacks onto the round bleached-oak pedestal table that was just large enough for two spindle-back chairs. "There are only two bedrooms, two baths, the living room, the kitchen and that tiny laundry room that leads to the garage." She pointed to her left where the washing machine and dryer could be seen through the connecting doorway. "I didn't think I'd end up here for any extended period of time, so when my ex-husband wanted me to find a house to buy for us to use whenever we visited, I just looked for something that offered the bare necessities."

"Why not stay with family when you visited?"

Boone asked, seeming far more at ease than she felt as she went for plates and utensils and then opened cartons of food.

"My ex-husband refused. Oddly enough, we lived with his family in Connecticut the rest of the time, but he said the only way he was coming here was if we had somewhere to stay that *wasn't* with my family. Then again, he only came with me twice, anyway. But I guess it's good that I have the place now."

She sorted through what she'd ordered, trying to figure out what was what. Boone had eaten at the restaurant in the past so he helped before settling on his favorites while Faith took a spoonful from each carton in order to validate her story about ordering so much so she could try a little of everything.

She also poured them both glasses of iced tea before they began to eat.

"If it's good that you have the house now does that mean that you're going to give in to your sisters and stay in Northbridge?" Boone asked.

"I'm here for now but I don't know about forever. I have a new apartment in Connecticut that I could go back to, too, if I decided that's what I want. Not because I hate it here or anything, though," she was quick to add. Then she smiled slyly and said, "Or because I'm high and mighty or have my nose in the air."

Boone pretended outrage. "Who said that about you? Anybody I know? I'll knock 'em flat for you."

Faith laughed, glad he'd played along. But she used the joke as a springboard anyway. "That stuff honestly isn't—and never was—true," she said because it bothered her to have just moments earlier seen that he was still leery of her and she wanted to explain herself once and for all.

"What's the truth, then?" he challenged.

"It's the reverend's fault."

The reverend—her grandfather—had met the majority of Northbridge's spiritual needs for decades before his retirement only a few years ago, so Faith knew there was no need to qualify who the reverend was to Boone.

"It was the reverend's fault?" Boone repeated as Faith paused to eat a bite of Mongolian beef.

"It wasn't that I hated Northbridge or anybody in it," she said when she'd finished her taste of the spicy meat, reiterating what she'd told him the day before. "I was just dying for more than I could get here and while some of that craving was just me and wanting what I was naturally drawn to, I think some of it was a result of being deprived of those things because the reverend wouldn't allow them."

Boone raised a forkful of crispy orange shrimp. "You wanted more than Chinese food and pizza delivered to your door?" he asked before taking a bite.

"When I left Northbridge you couldn't get *any-thing* delivered to your door. But that wasn't what I was thinking about."

"What *were* you thinking about?" he asked as if he was genuinely interested and open to what she was revealing about herself.

"The reverend was the high-and-mighty one in our family. He was the boss. My dad and my uncle Carl never stood up to him, so what the reverend said was law—"

"I don't think I've ever heard any one of you call him anything but *the reverend*—why is that?"

Faith shrugged. "Even my father and uncle call him the reverend. I don't know if it's the way he wanted it or if it just happened. I only know that I've never heard anyone call him *Dad* or *Grandpa* or anything…fond."

Boone nodded. "Yeah, he doesn't invite much warmth or closeness. Or give it."

"Or even allow it," Faith admitted. "In fact, he shuns it. Just try giving him a hug."

"No thanks," Boone said. "So okay, go on with what you were saying."

"Well, part of what the reverend demanded of us was that we live sparely. Essentials only. No luxuries. Bare-bones. We had nothing more than the families in his congregation who were struggling the most. I suppose it was an admirable sentiment but doing it the way he was determined it be done cut out a lot."

Boone seemed to think about that. "I never noticed, but now that I think about it, there wasn't anything flashy about you guys."

"Flashy? Hardly. Try dour and drab and dull. Only the oldest kids or the biggest got new clothes. The rest of us had to wear hand-me-downs until there was nothing left of them, and then we just got more hand-me-downs. Colors had to be bland, voices had to be soft, energies had to be spent solely in useful pursuits, life had to be spare and self-sacrificing to build character."

"Not a lot of fun," Boone said.

"Also not a lot of the things I loved—like art and music. To the reverend those were wastes of time, they meant idleness and idleness was never okay. But to me, they were important. They were what I wanted to learn about, to see and hear and experience—as I said, maybe more so because the reverend denied them. But it wasn't that I thought I was better than anybody around here, I just wanted what I hadn't been able to have, what I couldn't get here."

"So you had to get out."

"I wanted to be where there were art museums and galleries. Where there was opera and the symphony. Where there was ballet and theater—"

Faith stopped, afraid that to rough-and-tumble Boone this might only be confirming his opinion of her.

"It wasn't that I thought I was better than anyone,"

she continued. "I just craved something different than what I could have here. I'm not sure why that translated to you the way it did, but you've had me wrong all this time."

He studied her for a moment as if he was making a real attempt to see her through new eyes.

Then he said, "I guess what I thought of you *did* come from my own assumptions from a distance. Although there was that land-of-hayseeds remark," he reminded, this time teasing her.

"Teenage glibness. I was probably just trying to sound cool. But I'm really not some kind of snob."

He smiled in a way that cautioned in advance that he was about to goad her. "I'll believe that when I see you in a pair of jeans."

Faith rolled her eyes. "I didn't know there were fashion police in Northbridge," she countered.

He laughed. "That's me—chief of fashion police ordering you to relax a little and get comfortable."

"I might be able to do that if you stopped making me feel like some kind of three-eyed monster who's landed on your private territory. This is where I came from, too, if you'll recall. I was born and raised here just like you."

"Okay, okay, okay. I'll give you a break."

"That's big of you. Now who's being high and mighty?"

He laughed again, enjoying himself. "All right,

from here on let's make a pact—no more precon-
ceived notions. We'll just take it as it comes and get
to know each other."

"Deal," Faith said. "And no more high-and-
mighty anything."

"Deal," Boone agreed.

"Good," Faith said with relief. She had the sense
that they really *had* reached a turning point that
would allow them to move out from under the cloud
that had hung over them since Sunday.

"So," she said as a segue. "Tell me about the emergency that kept you out of your office all day."

"A difficult birth," he said as he pushed away his
plate, obviously finished eating but willing to sit back
and just chat to make good on their agreement to get
to know each other.

"Cow? Horse? Pig? Person?" Faith asked.

"I don't deliver human babies. This was a calf.
From the Vincoves' prize-winning cow inseminated
with sperm from this year's NILE stock show blue-
ribbon bull. There were complications and I had to
stay with her."

And had likely needed a shower afterward, no
matter who he'd been coming to see…

"Did it go all right?" Faith asked, trying not to
think about the fact that through a day like that she
likely couldn't have haunted his thoughts anywhere
near the way he'd haunted hers.

"It was touch and go for a while, but cow and calf ended up okay. Luckily for the Vincoves, because they nearly hocked their house to afford that sperm."

Faith flashed to how her mother-in-law would have responded to dinner talk that involved the word *sperm*. She wasn't altogether at ease with it herself, but that had more to do with what it was prompting in her own mind as she looked at Boone Pratt....

Another variation in subject seemed wise.

"And you had Charlie at the farm with you all day?" she asked.

"I did."

"How did you get any work done with her underfoot and barking and...well, being Charlie?" Faith asked with a nod at the insistent pooch nudging her leg for another bite of food.

"I didn't have any problems with her."

"Did you have to keep her on a leash the whole time?"

"No, she stayed close and came whenever I called her. The Vincoves have kids who kept an eye on her, too. But she was fine. She hung out with the Vincoves' dogs, got a swipe in the nose to teach her to steer clear of the cat, chased the chickens— she was fine."

"Charlie? *My* Charlie was off-leash and didn't run away and got along with kids and other animals?"

Maybe the fact that they were talking about her

prompted it, but all of a sudden Charlie leaped into Faith's lap, sending the table and everything on it rocking.

Boone barely caught his iced tea glass before it fell over and luckily when Faith's glass toppled only ice spilled.

"Charlie's middle name is Trouble," Faith said, before noticing that her remorseless pet was eating from her plate. "Oh, Charlie, no, don't do that!"

"Charlie, down," Boone commanded and, once more to Faith's shock, her dog jumped off her lap.

"Now sit," he added.

And again Charlie complied.

"How do you keep doing that? She never even listens to me let alone minds me."

Before answering her, Boone praised Charlie. "Good dog," he said calmly, rubbing the animal's head. Then he glanced from Charlie to Faith. "I'm the boss," he said simply but with enough confident authority that Faith certainly didn't doubt it.

She did, however, find something very sexy about it.

But she tamped down on that and said, "I've taken Charlie to more training classes than I can tell you and nothing works with her."

"That's because she has you trained more than you have her trained."

"The dog has trained me?"

"Pretty well from the looks of it," Boone said, barely suppressing a laugh.

"So this is my fault and not that Charlie is just a *bad dog?*" Faith whispered *bad dog* so as not to hurt Charlie's feelings.

Boone must have known what was behind her confidential tone and he couldn't stop a chuckle. "Charlie is a perfect example of her breed owned by a soft touch like you."

"I've gone from high-and-mighty, nose-in-the-air to soft touch now?"

With his blue eyes unwaveringly on hers, he said, "I thought we were done with high-and-mighty?"

"Right. Okay then, now I'm just a soft touch?" she amended.

"You are. You're every schnauzer's dream owner because they love to get away with murder. But if you keep at it you're going to end up hating your dog because Charlie will run right over you and eventually she'll turn into a bad dog."

The man did not mince words.

And although Faith adored her pet, Charlie often frustrated her enough that what Boone was predicting did not seem beyond the realm of possibility.

"So I need to be trained by someone other than my dog," Faith summarized.

Boone laughed again. "That's about it, yeah. Charlie is a dog, not a child. Dogs have packs and you're Charlie's pack. There has to be a leader of the pack and if you're not going to be it, she is."

"And with you?"

"I'm the leader of the pack. I let her know that and she does what I tell her to do."

Another helping of that quiet macho confidence that was more alluring than Faith wanted it to be.

But again she tried not to focus on that and reminded herself that it was Charlie she needed to be thinking about.

"Could you train me?" she asked Boone.

His grin was deliciously evil and obviously stemmed from something racy running through his head.

"To be leader of Charlie's pack," Faith added.

"I could," he said.

"Would you?" she asked because that didn't seem to be a foregone conclusion.

He didn't immediately answer, seeming to consider it for a time before he said, "Sure. How about tomorrow night after office hours? Out at my place? I'll even make you dinner to pay you back for this." He nodded in the direction of the remnants of their meal.

It seemed like quite a leap, though, from teaching her how to control her dog to inviting her over for dinner.

Was he turning her request into a date?

Maybe no more than she'd turned tonight into one, she told herself. And even if, along the way, this had begun to feel a little like a date, that *wasn't* what she'd intended it to be, so maybe that wasn't his intention, either.

Which was good because she wasn't ready to date. Or interested in it. Not until she knew what she was doing with herself, with her life, with her future. Not until she got herself together. And likely she wouldn't be dating anyone in Northbridge once that happened.

But if she went to Boone's house the next night to have him teach her how to control her dog and had dinner with him again just to even the score, it was only her and her dog's vet consulting on the matter of her pet's bad behavior. And if they threw in a meal, well, that's what happened in Northbridge—hometown hospitality.

Still, she felt obliged to say, "You don't have to do dinner."

"I have to eat one way or another. You might as well eat with me and then we'll be even."

"Otherwise you'll feel as if you owe me?" she joked.

"And I hate to be indebted."

Faith smiled at their rationalizations but by then she knew she was going to accept his invitation. Both because she needed the guidance with Charlie and because she wanted to—just on a friendly basis.

"Okay," she finally conceded.

"Can we leave the time open, though? I'll be swamped fitting in the appointments I missed today with the ones scheduled for tomorrow. I doubt that I'll get out of the office too early. Can I call you in the afternoon to let you know when it looks like I'll be finished?"

"Sure. I'm swamped, too, trying to throw a flea market together in such a rush. So if I'm not here when you call, just leave me a message."

"Anytime tomorrow evening is all right?"

"I'll be working up to the minute no matter what time it is."

"Good," he said, standing. "I should get going now, though. I told the Vincoves I'd stop by again tonight just to make sure everything's okay out there."

He started to clear the table but Faith assured him she'd take care of it, that he could go back to the Vincoves' cow.

Boone didn't put up much of a fight, saying he would already be getting there later than he'd promised.

As Faith followed him to the door she couldn't help catching a glimpse of his rear end in those jeans. And if nothing before had convinced her of the value of a pair of blue jeans, that did. In fact, if the man never wore anything else she couldn't imagine complaining about it.

Then they reached her door and he opened it, turning to her with his hand on the knob.

"Thanks for the Chinese food."

"Thanks for everything you did with Charlie."

Who had followed them to the door, too, but sat primly watching the proceedings after nothing more than one warning glance from Boone.

"Just doin' my job," he said.

Why was there something as sexy in that dropped *G* as there had been in his confidence with her dog?

Faith had no answer to that question, but the simple slang sent a little twitter through her anyway.

And it wasn't helped by Boone seeming to be in no hurry to leave now. He was standing there, gazing down at her from only a foot or so away, just like he might have if this *had* been a date and now they were saying good-night.

It had been a long time since Faith had dated but still she recognized what one felt like at this point, when she would be wondering if he was going to kiss her or not.

And if this *had* been a date and she *were* wondering if he was going to kiss her or not, would she want him to?

Maybe…

But this wasn't a date, she reminded herself in a silent but firm inner voice.

And yet she tipped her chin in a way that was almost a hint as her gaze seemed to home in—all on its own—on his supple-looking lips. Lips that could have been poised for kissing because there was the tiniest gap between the two.

Go ahead….

He seemed to lean forward. But barely a fraction of an inch.

Or maybe not. Maybe she only thought he had.

But he wasn't saying good-night, either. He wasn't taking those cool blue eyes off of her. He wasn't making any move to leave....

As if it were connected to puppet strings, Faith's chin raised another notch and rather than looking at his mouth alone, now she took in all of that handsome, handsome face.

Really, go ahead....

But he didn't.

And when he muttered a plain, "See you tomorrow night," and finally left, Faith didn't have a clue if he'd been thinking about kissing her or if she'd been the only one of them entertaining the idea.

He was gone before she realized she hadn't answered his parting words. Worried he might have seen that oversight as snobbery again, as if she'd thought she was too good to answer him, she stepped onto her porch just as he was backing his truck out of her driveway, and waved.

But she didn't know if he saw her because in the middle of it Charlie came out the front door and Faith barely caught her before the dog could jump off the porch to make a run for it.

Faith scooped the dog into her arms and straightened up, but by then Boone was driving down her street.

"Thanks a lot, Charlie Trouble," she said as she took the dog back inside and closed the door behind them.

That was when she realized that Charlie smelled faintly of Boone's cologne.

She pressed her nose to the top of the schnauzer's head and closed her eyes, instantly picturing Boone as clearly as if he were still there with her, still looking into her eyes, still maybe going to kiss her....

But he hadn't and she wondered why Boone's *not* kissing her made her feel as if she'd been denied something. Something she hadn't even known she wanted.

That was how she felt, though.

"It's just silly," she said, opening her eyes and kissing Charlie's flopped-over ear instead.

But when she did she caught another whiff of Boone's cologne.

And silly or not, she was still wishing it wasn't the dog she was kissing.

Chapter Four

"Wine and review. Here's your wine, now tell me what you learned."

Faith accepted the glass of wine that Boone poured and handed to her, complying with his demand that she repeat all he'd taught her in the last hour about how to handle Charlie.

"I'm the leader of the pack," Faith recited. "Anytime Charlie tries to be, I need to dominate her by getting on the ground, holding her to lie on her side until she stops fighting me, lays her head down, relaxes and submits. Short, straightforward commands—no begging or pleading or asking her to do what I want her to do. Calm but firm voice. Let her know her boundaries. Enforce them. Lots of praise and rewards and treats for doing what she's supposed to."

"Not a lot of that, no," Boone corrected. "Some. But primarily you want her to know that behaving is what's expected of her and meeting those expectations is what she's to do—plain and simple. In the wild, the alpha dog wouldn't go all cream puff on her or toss her a bit of liver every time she does what she's supposed to do."

"I'm not a cream puff and Charlie likes her treats," Faith defended.

"Faith…" Boone said in the same tone he used to warn Charlie.

Faith laughed. "I know—if I let her call the shots, she will."

"Good girl," he praised, again as if she were the dog, but only teasingly.

"Now where's my liver?" she joked.

"No liver. You'll have to settle for mesclun-stuffed pink trout basted in herbs and white wine and cooked in parchment paper."

"If that's the best you can do," Faith said with a sigh when, in actuality, she'd been wondering about the wonderful aroma filling the kitchen. The last thing she'd thought she'd be served tonight was gourmet food.

But then nothing she'd found at Boone's ranch was what she'd expected.

"I need to tweak a few things in here. Why don't you take our appetizers into the living room and I'll be out in a minute," Boone suggested, handing her a tray of what looked like tiny, golden-brown puff-pastry pouches that he'd said were filled with portobello mushroom tapenade.

"You're sure I can't help you do something?" she offered for the third time.

"I'm sure. Just go sit and watch your dog being part of my dogs' pack."

Faith took her wine and the tray, passing under the wide archway that connected the living room. Charlie was indeed there, lying among Boone's assortment of dogs: two Labradors, a German shepherd, a greyhound and a mutt that had a face like a terrier, curly hair and a long tail.

It was after eight o'clock on Wednesday evening. Faith had been at Boone's place since six-thirty when they'd arrived at the sprawling ranch at the same time. He'd called that afternoon and said he thought he'd make it home by six, that she could come half an hour later. But he'd been detained at his office at the last minute and hadn't gotten there ahead of her.

As a result, Faith had been on her own while he'd showered. He'd told her to make herself at home, to get herself something to drink, but she'd stayed in the living room rather than forage through his kitchen for a glass or a beverage. Beyond checking out the eclectic music, video and book collections that were prominently displayed on open shelves, she hadn't wanted to snoop.

Well, she'd *wanted* to, but she hadn't.

Still, even those surface appearances were enough to kick off an evening of surprises.

She'd been in this house when it had belonged to the Carlinger family so she knew what it had been like years ago—dumpy was her kindest description—but somewhere along the way it had been remodeled considerably. Now it had a sophisticated rustic-cabin feel that somehow managed to mingle with the casual style of log walls and raw-beamed ceilings, giving it a certain understated masculine sophistication.

Man-sized, butter-soft brown leather furniture co-existed with Tiffany lamps. A state-of-the-art entertainment center was tucked beneath a rack of antlers. The hardwood floor was left scarred under the varnish and covered in the center with a handmade Native American rug.

The kitchen, too, managed a country hominess despite the modern appliances that would be any chef's dream come true.

And while she had no idea if Boone had had anything to do with the improvements, it was where he lived and it was not how she'd pictured it. Especially when he'd told her on the phone today that he was on the old Carlinger property. She'd imagined the awful place with eleven more years of decay and neglect, and put him in the middle of it.

When he'd rejoined her after his shower she'd refrained from commenting about the differences. Instead, she let him take her on a tour of the rest of the house and the property, which included a modern barn where his own horses were stalled alongside the rescued horses in four-star equine luxury.

"How're my pockets?" Boone called from the kitchen.

What flashed through Faith's mind were the pockets of the jeans he'd changed into when he'd emerged from his after-work shower. They fit him exactly the way jeans should—and not at all like jeans had fit her ex-husband on the two occasions when he'd come to Northbridge and worn them. To *rough it,* as he'd said. On her ex-husband, jeans looked as foreign as an ill-conceived Halloween costume, while Boone wore them as if he'd been born to them. And as she'd followed him on the ranch tour she'd had trouble keeping her eyes off his rear pockets and the backside they encased.

But now it occurred to her that he was referring to his hors d'oeuvres as pockets.

"I haven't tried them. I'm waiting for you," she

answered, tamping down the image of her slipping her hands into his jean pockets to try *them* out.

Thoughts like that had been assaulting her since the night before. She didn't know why, but she'd decided it must be the country air that was causing her the girlish, romantic delirium.

She'd also decided that that was what had been going on with her the previous evening when she'd walked Boone to the door. That *that* was the reason kissing had been on her mind, the reason she'd imagined—and she'd convinced herself she *had* only imagined it—that he might have leaned forward as if he were on the verge of actually doing the deed.

She'd told herself firmly on the way to his ranch that she needed to put every effort into controlling her wayward thoughts. Under no circumstances was she to believe there was any substance to them or that anything would come of them.

"Okay, here I am. Try one," Boone said as he joined her in the living room, carrying his own glass of wine.

Faith took a deep breath, straightened her spine to strengthen her resolve not to slip into fantasies and chose a bite-sized delicacy to nibble.

It was wonderful and she did let him know it. Then she took a sip of wine, recognizing it when she did.

"I know this wine," she said, surprised yet again. "I love it." Her former husband had a case of it that he kept in his private reserve for special occasions because it was pricey and relatively rare. "You know your wines," she marveled.

Boone raised one eyebrow and his glass but he didn't confirm or deny it. Then he took an appetizer and sat at the opposite end of the couch, lounging back comfortably while Faith sat primly on the edge of the cushion at the other end, realizing only then that her dog wasn't begging at her feet, yet another novelty.

"I think this is the first time I've ever had food anywhere around you-know-who and she's stayed away," Faith whispered to Boone so as not to rouse Charlie's interest.

"I don't allow begging here," Boone responded in a normal octave. "She'll do as much as you'll let her get away with."

"So the begging is my fault, too?"

"Sorry, but yes, it is."

He was wearing a blue-and-black western-style shirt—not Faith's taste, but she had to admit that, on him, it looked good. Especially with the long sleeves rolled to his elbows. The man had the sexiest hands, wrists and forearms she'd ever seen.

He was also freshly shaven, his too-long hair—which she was finding uncharacteristically attractive as well—waved away from his stare-worthy face, and he smelled of that same cologne she'd savored with every breath she took when he'd sat across from her, eating Chinese takeout.

But she couldn't just sit there ogling him out of the corner of her eye, so she opted for talking about his house.

"This place doesn't look at all like it did when the Carlingers had it."

"Yeah, I got a good deal on it because it was in such bad shape when I bought it from them."

"So you fixed it up—I wondered if someone else had had it between the Carlingers and you."

"Nope, just me. My brothers and I gutted the place and did most of the remodel. My sisters did the lion's share of the decorating for me because otherwise we'd probably be sitting on lawn chairs and using packing crates as end tables."

He took another of his appetizers then gave her a sly half smile and said, "Lawn chairs and packing crates—I'll bet that's the way you figured I'd be living, isn't it? And probably—if you gave it any thought at all—you figured I'd be at Mara's and Jared's wedding with a big potbelly busting open the buttons of a dress shirt with ketchup stains on the front of it."

"No, I didn't think that," she said defensively even though she sort of had. "But I've kept some boxes of old things stored at my house and today I dug out my yearbook to look you up. You have to admit, this house isn't the only thing that's undergone a transformation."

"*Transformation?* I don't know if I'd go *that* far."

Looking at him now, Faith didn't think transformation was too strong a word. Not when she mentally compared the big, buff, bodaciously handsome man to the pudgy, babyfaced graduation picture. "It's hard to believe that you and the boy in that yearbook picture are the same person."

"Yeah, well, fixing up this place took a lot of work. Luckily I didn't."

"Seriously?" she said, having thought that the hard, expansive muscles he was sporting had come from some concentrated effort. "You didn't join a gym or go on an all-protein diet or start running marathons?"

He shook his head. "Northbridge doesn't have a gym, I eat what I want and I don't have time for running marathons. I told you, I just had a growth spurt first year of college."

"Overnight you went from the way you looked in high school to the way you do now?"

"It didn't happen overnight, no. But through that year I grew like a weed and that stretched out the flab."

"And you didn't start lifting weights or anything?"

"I lift bales of hay and buckets of feed and water. I dig trenches and postholes. I shovel snow. Around here, everyday living is a workout."

A workout that worked.

But Faith didn't say that.

"What was it like to go from being the way you were to the way you are now *almost* overnight?"

"Are you kidding? It was great," he said with a laugh, eating a third mushroom bundle.

Faith laughed, too. "Did you have girls suddenly falling all over you?"

"Falling all over me? Nah. The outside changed but in my head I was still a supergeek—it wasn't as if I'd developed any kind of flirting or talking-to-girls skills. Or even basic social skills. Besides, to tell you the truth, that first year I was more the town freak show. I couldn't go anywhere without everybody making comments about how fast I was growing, how big I was getting—as if I were eight years old. And you know the way it goes around here—folks get started on something and they can run it into the ground. That year, my growth spurt had them all watching me. There were half a dozen places where they'd measure me every time I walked in the door— that part was not so great."

"No, I don't imagine it was. When did they get over it?"

"I transferred to Colorado State University in Fort Collins after my first year of college in town. I was hoping that I'd have a better chance of getting into the vet school if I did my undergrad there. I had my first real date then—I guess it was easier with girls who only knew the *after* without having known the *before*. That was when it was great…." he said, innuendo lacing his tone. "Anyway, I came back here for holidays and folks would see me and we'd go through the whole look-how-you've-grown routine again, but it dwindled. By the time I finished school and bought out old Doc Chapman's practice my *transformation* stopped being an issue. Until now," he said pointedly.

A timer went off in the kitchen just then and Boone got to his feet. "Soup's on!" he announced.

Faith trailed behind with her wine and the appetizers, not trusting Charlie with an unattended plate, no matter whose house this was.

A large rectangular table took up one end of the kitchen and a much smaller island counter stood in the center with bar stools around it. When she'd been sent to the living room neither the table nor the island had been set for dining. Apparently that was part of the tweaking Boone had needed to do because now there were two places set on the island.

"The table's too formal. I thought we'd eat here," Boone explained as he filled a serving bowl from a pan on the stove and put it between the mats and silverware that were on the butcher's block.

"Take a seat," he instructed as he removed a cookie sheet from the oven.

Faith set her wineglass and the remaining appetizers on the island and then climbed onto one of the tall bar stools. She immediately pulled the cloth napkin from her place setting and opened it onto her lap to protect her trouser-cut jeans. They were the only kind of jeans she owned and still made her look more like she belonged in Connecticut than in Montana.

It was warm in the kitchen and she unfastened the French cuffs of her white blouse and rolled up her sleeves much the way Boone's were. She watched him tear parchment paper and adeptly transfer two stuffed fish to waiting dinner plates.

"The trout is boned, so you don't have to worry about that," he informed her as he placed one dish in front of her and the other at his setting. "And that—" he pointed to the bowl between them "—is wild rice with saffron. I didn't make a salad because of the greens stuffed in the fish, but if you want one—"

"This is plenty. And amazing. Have you always been a gourmet cook?"

"Gourmet? Me? Nah."

"I don't know," she teased him. "Maybe you're just hiding behind all this cowboy stuff."

"Don't kid yourself. I still like watching a good rodeo or an old Western movie and I can toss back beers and hot wings with the best of 'em."

She didn't doubt that and she knew it was something she needed to keep in mind.

"I just like to eat," he continued. "And in college I had to learn a few things to feed myself. Since I also like to fish, I have a freezer full of trout. I can fix it about any way you can think of."

Faith took some of the rice, tasted both the entrée and the side dish and decided that while Boone might not want the title of gourmet, he deserved it. She told him so, but he waved away the notion.

"This must have taken some preparation and we both got here at the same time tonight. When did you do it?" she asked.

"I came home at lunch, grabbed a bite to eat—some beef jerky, in case you're thinking I'm too far from being a caveman—and got everything ready."

"Dog training and delicious food—all you got out of me last night was Chinese takeout."

"Okay, I'm showing off a little," he confessed. "But you can think of it as incentive to raise a ton of money for the horse rescue."

"After this, I'll have to," Faith said, wondering why he'd wanted to show off for her.

But she wasn't going to find out because he changed the subject.

"Did you say you'd just come from having lunch with Celeste today when I called?" he asked.

The phone had been ringing when Faith had unlocked her front door this afternoon. Rushing to answer it had left her sounding harried.

"Eve, Eden and I took her to lunch at Adz," she confirmed. "We want to get to know her as more than just the lady who worked at your family's dry cleaners."

"How's that going?"

"Pretty well, I think. It was awkward when I was here in January, but it's better now. I never realized before how close Celeste was to you all—she was talking about that today. It sounds like she's been more your grandmother than mine."

"My mother hired her at the dry cleaners when she first snuck back into town—not knowing who she was, of course."

After leaving Northbridge, Faith's long-lost grandmother had undergone a transformation of her own. She'd gained so much weight that it had left her unrecognizable and able to return to town and secretly watch over the sons she'd deserted.

"Celeste and my mother became friends long before my mother married or had us," Boone went on. "She was a fixture at our house and we believed she didn't have anyone else. My mom always said that she wouldn't have lived through being left alone with seven kids when dear old Dad took off if it hadn't been for Celeste, and I don't know what we would have done without her when Mom went into kidney failure and then died. Celeste is a good person—no matter what rash act made her leave your grandfather."

"Ah, so you can forgive her but not me for wanting out of Northbridge," Faith accused.

He smiled. "I walked right into that one, didn't I?"

"Well?" Faith challenged.

"Yeah, okay," he conceded. "And I guess at the bottom of it was the same thing—the reverend and wanting to escape what he was forcing on you both." Then Boone's smile turned sly. "But Celeste had the good sense to come back to Northbridge. The jury is still out about whether or not you've wised up enough to stick around."

Faith laughed. "Would that redeem me?"

"If it happens I'll let you know."

Faith laughed again and rolled her eyes at him.

They'd finished eating and she was too full for the ice cream he offered for dessert. He decided to pass it up, too, and didn't balk at her insistence that she help clean the dinner mess.

As they got started on that Boone said, "So, did you get all that art and music and opera and ballet you were after when you left?"

"I did. I also got my own education and met the kind of people I'd wanted to meet."

Boone looked up from loading the dishwasher and frowned. "Meaning what? Rich people?"

"I didn't care about anybody's bank account," she said. "It was culture I wanted. To go to galleries and museums, to concerts and the opera and the ballet, with people who appreciated it the way I do, who could talk about it. Who could talk about books and literature and something that didn't involve crop or cattle prices and what kind of winter we were in for."

"I don't know," he said as if she were trying to put something over on him. "From what I've heard you went off to play with the rich kids. *Faith married money*—that's something the whole town's pretty clear on."

"Money did seem to go with the territory, yes. Plus, after I graduated with a business degree and became an event and party planner, my clients tended to be wealthy. As time went by that was just the circle I was in, but it wasn't as if it was what I was looking for."

"You didn't *plan* to marry money—is that what you're getting at?"

"It wasn't what I was *getting at,* but no, I didn't *plan* to marry money. And I didn't. I married a man who happened to have money," Faith said, not denying what she knew was common knowledge. She also knew that the fact that the marriage had ended in divorce was widely known. But outside of close friends in Connecticut, only her family was aware of the details of the divorce, and it was nothing she intended to talk about now with Boone.

She readied herself for having to tell him as much. But maybe he sensed that she'd reached the end of her willingness to talk about her failed marriage because rather than pursuing anything else in that direction, he said, "You got out of Northbridge, you got the music, art and culture you wanted—was it as good as you thought it would be?"

"It was," she said.

"It was all good and now you're back here—that doesn't make it seem like I should put my money on you staying."

Did that matter to him? It almost sounded as if it might and yet Faith couldn't believe that it would.

"I said the music, art and culture were as good as I thought they would be," she amended. "Unfortunately some bad came with the good and so it wasn't *all* good."

"Was the bad bad enough to keep you away from the good for good?"

Faith laughed at his wordplay and answered him honestly. "I don't know. Not everything was the way it looked. The way I thought it was. And now…" She shrugged. "Now I'm just trying to figure things out for myself."

They'd finished the cleanup and since what she'd come here for tonight was over, it seemed like the evening should be, too. And because she certainly didn't want to overstay her welcome, she said, "It's getting late. Charlie and I should go."

Not that she wanted to, as she discovered the minute she made the suggestion. In fact, she'd been enjoying everything about this evening and she was in no hurry for it to end.

But Boone accepted her declaration and she had to follow through.

"This was nice," she told him as they went out to the living room again where Faith had left her purse.

"And you only sound a little surprised," he joked.

This time Faith opted not to make any attempt to refute that as she put the strap of her purse over her shoulder and glanced at Charlie, expecting her dog to get up and be eager to go the way she usually was. But the schnauzer was happily snoozing with the other canines and didn't even notice her.

"Looks like Charlie has taken up permanent residence," Faith observed.

"Just call her."

"Charlie, come," Faith complied. And up popped Charlie.

"See? She's still your dog," Boone said.

"Think I should put the leash on her to get her out to the car?"

"She'll be fine without it. Don't take her into town without one, but she'll be okay here." Then, as they reached the front door, he said, "I'll show you the safest way for her to ride if she isn't in a crate."

"There are rules for that, too? I've had her for almost a whole year and I never knew."

"It's not law or anything, just a safety precaution."

Faith hadn't locked her car when she'd arrived and Boone went to the passenger side, opened the door and instructed Charlie to get in, then told her to get on the floor in front of the seat.

"Down there?" Faith said. "That seems mean—she can't see out the window."

It was Boone's turn to roll his eyes as he closed the door. "It's for her own good," he said. "That's where she rode with me in my truck and she never filed a complaint, so I think we're okay."

Faith thought he would say good-night and go into the house, but he followed her around the rear of the sedan and opened her door, too.

"Thanks," she said, stepping into the lee of the door but not getting into the vehicle yet, facing Boone where he stood a scant foot away. "And thanks for dinner, too. It was fabulous. You can be my cook anytime—"

She cut herself off, worrying that he might take it the wrong way.

Which he did, but he still didn't seem offended when he said, "If I ever need a second job I'll send in my application to be your personal chef."

"I'll leave word with the butler to hire you on the spot," she said facetiously in return.

As she looked up into his handsome face gilded in the creamy light of the moon, she reminded herself that she wasn't going to read anything into the fact that he seemed to be lingering there. It hadn't meant anything the night before and it probably didn't mean anything tonight.

But she didn't say a quick goodbye, either. She stayed where she was.

"Does Charlie need a follow-up visit or stitches removed or anything?" she asked, looking for any excuse to prolong things.

"The stitches will dissolve and unless she starts having problems, there's no reason for me to see her again."

Or to see me, either…

It was insane how much that disappointed her.

Faith took a deep breath and then sighed, hoping her disappointment didn't show. "Well, then, thanks for all that, too—Charlie's tooth and taking care of her."

Boone nodded but he didn't say anything. He merely stood there studying her, making her worry that she was wearing her feelings on her face. Feelings not only about Boone and how much she was thinking about him kissing her, but also feelings that came from wondering if he would ever want to kiss her. Or if for some reason she was incapable of inspiring that in him the way she'd been incapable of inspiring it in her disinterested ex…

"You're a little raw around the edges, aren't you," he said then, making it clear that she'd given herself away.

She shrugged again but only with one shoulder, not wanting to admit too much.

"You are. I can see it."

"If you give me grief about running home to

Northbridge with my tail between my legs I swear I'll punch you."

The grin that stretched across his face was slow, but there was only kindness and sympathy in his expression.

"Nah, home is where we're supposed to go when life hits us hard. It's good you're here."

Faith had no idea why, but his saying that sent a wave of relief and gratitude through her.

Not wanting him to know how much impact something so simple could have on her when it came from him, she said, "I'd better go."

She finally got into the car and when she did, Boone stepped forward to close her door.

But she hadn't said good-night so she pushed the button to lower the window after she started the engine.

He must have taken that as an invitation because he grasped the top of the door with both hands and bent low enough to bring his face near as she turned hers into the frame.

"It'll be okay, you know," he said.

Faith nodded. "Sure," she agreed without much conviction.

"Trust me."

She laughed and it made him smile sheepishly. And very endearingly.

"Yeah, I know," he said. "Why should you trust anything I say when I started out makin' things harder on you, right? When I acted as if you didn't have any business coming back here? Well, trust me anyway. I'd never lead you astray."

"Too bad," she joked before she even knew she was going to say anything, let alone something that full of insinuation.

Still, it broadened his smile into a grin again, letting her know he'd liked it. "Well, maybe not *never*," he said with some insinuation of his own.

For another moment his too-beautiful-to-belong-to-a-man blue eyes delved into hers and then, without warning, he tipped his head to one side, poked it through the window and kissed her.

Just once. Just lightly. Just briefly.

Just not enough…

Before he retreated.

"Always wanted to do that," he said.

One last surprise.

"You did?"

But once more Boone didn't answer her. He only smiled an enigmatic smile, stood up straight and tapped the roof of her car.

"Drive safe," he ordered, leaving her no recourse but to put the car into gear and pull away.

But she was still thinking about that just-not-enough kiss and what he'd said after it.

He'd *always* wanted to do that? How far back did

always stretch? To when they were in school together and she'd barely known he'd existed?

And if that was the case, why hadn't he done it last night—when maybe he *had* leaned in a little and been thinking about kissing her as much as she'd been thinking about kissing him?

Or at least why hadn't he done it tonight before she'd gotten into the car? When he could have wrapped his arms around her? When he could have pulled her against him and really, really kissed her…

No, it was better that he hadn't, she told herself.

"This isn't why I came here and it will only confuse things!" she nearly shrieked, realizing only then that somewhere along the way, Charlie had hopped up onto the passenger seat in spite of Boone's efforts to teach them both how it *should* be done.

"Maybe you'd better tell me how you do that," she said to her dog, thinking that Charlie seemed to have no problem putting the effects of Boone Pratt behind her.

But putting the effects of Boone Pratt behind her was something Faith knew she needed to learn more than she needed to learn how to handle Charlie.

And fast.

Before she fell into something that she might not be able to get out of.

Chapter Five

"Boone—hold up a minute, will you?"

"Sure," Boone answered.

It was early Thursday evening and after finishing his office hours Boone had come to his family home. His sisters, Mara and Neily, still lived in the old house, but tonight he'd come to meet his brothers, his soon-to-be brother-in-law Jared Perry and Jared's brother, Noah. Business tycoon Jared Perry was marrying Mara on Sunday, and Jared had brought in his private tailor for the final fittings on the suits that had been made for them all for the occasion.

The fittings had just been completed and as

everyone got dressed in their own clothes they were filing downstairs where cold beer was waiting. Boone had no idea why Jared wanted him to hang back.

"Should you and I talk?" Jared asked when he and Boone were the only two left in the bedroom that—as one of a set of triplets—Boone had shared in his youth with his brothers Jon and Taylor. It was now a guest bedroom.

"Should we talk?" Boone reiterated, at a loss for what his sister's fiancé was getting at. "If you want," he said with a shrug as he propped his backside against the window ledge to pull the legs of his jeans over the tops of the cowboy boots he'd just put on. "What do you want to talk about?"

"In all the razzing that's been tossed at me here tonight you haven't said a word. I'm beginning to wonder if you have a problem with me marrying Mara."

"Oh, hell no," Boone said without hesitation, letting his tone of voice make it clear that was out of the question. And it was—Mara had sorted through her own qualms about Jared Perry's jet-setting life-style away from their small hometown and Boone had confidence in his sister's judgment. He also liked her fiancé. Jared might have left Northbridge behind, gone out and found a way to nearly own the world, but he was back now, building a big house on the out-skirts of town, and Boone thought he was a good guy.

"I don't have a problem with you and Mara getting married," Boone added just to make sure his almost-brother-in-law didn't go away believing otherwise. "I just have some things on my mind." Namely Faith. Whom he couldn't seem to get *off* his mind.

"Anything I can help with?" Jared asked. "I'm a problem solver now, you know," he joked, referring to the fact that he'd only recently gone from hostile takeovers to consulting ailing businesses on keeping them solvent.

But what was Boone going to say? That he was worried his old high school crush on Jared's cousin might be cropping up again to torment him? That he still couldn't believe he'd kissed her the night before even though he'd been thinking about kissing her almost obsessively and had inched his way toward doing it on Tuesday night before he'd caught himself? Was he going to tell Jared that no matter how hard he was fighting it—and he was fighting hard—he was finding himself attracted to her and he knew damn good and well that he had to stop it? That he didn't have to be told that eventually she was going to hightail it out of the small town that couldn't offer her what she wanted, and if he let himself get attached to her before that happened he was going to be sorry?

No, he couldn't say any of that.

So what he said was, "Thanks for the offer, but it's just something I have to work through."

Jared Perry nodded. "As long as nothing has gone wrong between you and me."

"Nah," Boone assured.

Apparently that convinced Jared, because as he shrugged into his shirt and began to button it, he let the subject drop and said, "I hear my cousin Faith had need of your services."

"Her dog Charlie broke a tooth," Boone confirmed, making certain to keep his tone neutral.

"Celeste said you were working with Faith to teach her how to train the dog, too."

Small town. Everyone knew everyone else's business. Boone was used to it.

"Yeah, at this point Charlie has the upper hand," Boone confirmed the gossip. Then, knowing he should mind his own business but unable to stop himself, he grasped the edges of the windowsill on either side of him to appear indifferent and said, "Have you seen a lot of Faith over the years?"

"Here and there. No more or less than the rest of the family."

"I thought maybe with the both of you living east…" Boone shrugged again. "I understand she married money and we all know you aren't hurtin' any—seems like that might have put you in with the same crowd."

"Not much, no. We were in the same area of the country but, until your sister reeled me in, I was such a workaholic that I didn't do much socializing in Connecticut where Faith was or even in New York where I was based. Besides, to tell you the truth, the family Faith married into could buy and sell me about three times over. And they're *old money*—that makes me an upstart in their eyes and not in any way in their league. So related to Faith or not, it wasn't as if I was on that particular A-list."

"But they accepted Faith all right?"

Jared didn't answer that too readily. "They…*conceded* to accept Faith." He said it in a way that made Boone's curiosity grow.

Then Jared added, "But Faith's a sweetheart and once she was part of the family she made the Fosters look good. They've had wealth and power for so long that they're like royalty—insulated, out of touch with what's beyond their own elite group. And they aren't known for their generosity or compassion. They're the let-them-eat-cake collective."

"And Faith was okay with *that?*"

"Faith made improvements in that. She kept up the Fosters' affiliation with the arts—which are the pretty and fun causes that they've always been involved in. But she also did a lot of charity work that the Fosters in general got credit for because, after all, she was a *Foster* when she was doing it. She organized fund-raisers for things that did some good for underprivileged and abused kids, for the homeless, for battered women—things the Fosters hadn't been connected with before. And as I said, that helped their image."

"Were they grateful for that?" Boone persisted, hoping he wasn't giving away just how much he wanted to know about her past.

"Let's just say they were luckier to have her than she was to have them."

Boone had no idea what that meant but he didn't feel free to ask for an explanation. What he did say, though, was, "*They. Them*—did she marry a guy or a conglomerate?"

"That's probably a question she asked herself more than once. Especially when it turned out that she was the sacrificial lamb," Jared answered as he stepped into his own shoes. Then, apparently at the end of his willingness to talk about his cousin, he headed for the bedroom door. "What do you say we go down and get a couple of those beers?"

"Right behind you," Boone said without abandoning the windowsill.

As Jared left him he was even more occupied with thoughts about Faith than he had been before.

Faith had been a sacrificial lamb?

What had Jared been alluding to? How had she been a sacrificial lamb and what had she been sacrificed for? And by whom, exactly? Her husband? His family? And if it was his family, why hadn't her husband stopped it? And what happened in the end to break them up?

The questions piled on top of each other.

But there was something else that disturbed him, too. Something he didn't understand.

Why did merely hearing what his soon-to-be brother-in-law had just said make him want to go out right this minute, find Faith and try to make it better somehow or protect her or get some revenge for her or…something?

It was none of his business, he told himself. It certainly wasn't his issue. It wasn't anything he should care about one way or another.

But that was the trouble.

He *did* care.

More than he should.

Already.

On every front.

Which brought him back to what he'd been fretting about since that kiss last night—was his old crush on her rearing its ugly head again? That infatuation that had turned him upside down and inside out without anyone ever even knowing?

Because that wouldn't do anyone any good.

So no, he certainly wasn't going out right this minute looking for Faith as if he were some damn knight on a white charger.

And he wasn't going to kiss her again, either.

He was just going to keep his distance. Then maybe he could get a handle on this damn attraction before it went any further.

Faith was in town to heal—no matter what she said, that's what he believed.

And once she did, she'd leave again—he was convinced of that, too.

The last thing he wanted when that happened was to be here, sitting on another secret crush that did nothing but make him miserable.

Faith attended Thursday night's town meeting. After a lot of intense work since early Monday morning—and with the help of her sisters, her cousins, numerous volunteers and the town council itself—tables and awnings had already been set up in the town square, signs had been posted and ads had been placed. But the town meeting was the perfect venue in which to answer questions and announce that donations would be accepted and sorted through as they came in tomorrow, so the mayor had convinced her to go.

Once the subject of the charity flea market was exhausted, Faith would have liked to leave. But the mayor announced that after the meeting she'd be available for more questions and now she was stuck. So she sat back in her seat in the center of the crowd in the meeting hall, despite having no interest in the rest of the open-forum assembly attended by most of the townspeople and paneled by the town council and the mayor.

"A car has been left parked in front of the ice-cream shop for at least two days now," the mayor announced as Faith spotted Boone standing against a side wall.

She hadn't seen him there before and wasn't sure when he'd arrived. And although she knew it should not have mattered to her, she was suddenly in less of a hurry to get away.

"It's an older model red station wagon," the mayor was saying, obviously reading the information for the first time from one of many sheets of paper in front of him on the podium. "It has Montana plates and is registered to a Mary-Pat Gordman, address in Missoula." The paunchy man looked out at his audience. "Any of that ring a bell with anybody?"

There were murmurs in the crowd but no one answered the question.

"Well, spread the word," he said. "Maybe it belongs to a houseguest of someone who isn't here tonight. We're also running a notice in tomorrow's newspaper, but if the car isn't claimed by Saturday morning we'll have to impound it."

The mayor riffled through his papers, then said, "That's about it for notices. I'll throw it open to you all, if there's anything you want to—"

"Has the Hobbs' house at the end of South Street been sold or rented?"

It was Boone who had spoken up and since that drew most eyes his way, Faith had good reason to look directly at him, too.

For a moment, anyway, before attention returned to the front where the mayor conferred with the town council. But she'd been able to look at Boone long enough to notice that he was dressed in jeans, a white Western shirt tucked into them, and that while again it wasn't her style, he looked rugged and sexy and outrageously good to her.

"No," the mayor finally announced in response to Boone's question. "Nothing's been done with that old relic."

"Then college kids must be partying in it again. When I've driven past it on my way home the last two nights I've seen lights in the downstairs windows and there's been smoke comin' out of the chimney," Boone said.

His deep voice washed over Faith like a balm and she wondered if everyone in the room responded to him that way or if it was only her. And if it *was* only her, why did she respond to it like that?

"Damn college kids," the mayor grumbled under his breath. "We'll have the police check it out and keep a closer eye on the place," he concluded. "Anything else?"

Other small matters were brought up and duly noted before the mayor went on to talk about the progress on the reconditioning of the north bridge. But the entire time Faith was more aware of Boone than of anything being said. And of the fact that he never once glanced in her direction.

Which was as it should have been, she told herself. They were, after all, merely two separate residents of the same place. Seeing each other every day since she'd been back didn't make them any more than that. And that kiss of the night before? That had merely been some kind of old business. *His* old business, not hers. It hadn't been the start of anything and she didn't want anything started anyway, so it was good that he didn't seem to even notice her, let alone be looking for her.

He'd had his hair cut, though, she noticed as her eyes darted in his direction on their own. It wasn't cut short—he'd taken off maybe half an inch all over—but enough so she could tell. He'd probably just had it cleaned up for the wedding on Sunday.

And it occurred to Faith as she kept stealing split-second glimpses of him that she was glad he hadn't had it cut more than that. She'd come to like his longer hair and couldn't imagine it shorter. It suited him.

The town meeting concluded then, with Faith having no recollection of anything that had been said at the end. Everyone stood and began to mill around and Faith was instantly overrun by people who just wanted to welcome her back to Northbridge or who wanted to assure her they would be bringing donations for the flea market or who wanted to ask if particular items would be welcome.

Through it, she lost sight of Boone.

He's probably gone home, she thought.

And there was no reason for him not to have gone, she told herself firmly. He'd come to ask about the Hobbs' house and once the meeting was over, he'd left—just the way he should have.

He didn't have to stay around just to say hello to me, for crying out loud.

And he hadn't.

Which was fine and exactly the way it should have been.

And she certainly wasn't going to let it ruin a perfectly nice evening….

It was well past ten o'clock before Faith managed to get away from chatting and answering questions after the town meeting. The weather had been so warm when she'd left home that she'd decided to walk the few blocks from her house, expecting that she'd be heading home much earlier. But when she stepped outside of the meeting hall she found the air much colder than she'd anticipated and not only didn't she have her car, she'd also only brought along her lightweight jacket.

As she crossed Main Street she slipped the jacket on over her twill slacks and silk blouse. She'd barely done that and reached the other side of the street when a vintage, apple-red sports car pulled up beside her.

"Where're your wheels, lady?"

The voice.

She knew even before she looked through the half-open window that it was Boone. He must have hung around somewhere outside of the town hall until now....

"Home," she answered his quip. "Where's that ratty old truck of yours?"

"You thought that was all I owned?" he challenged. "Well, this one's mine, too. I fixed her up myself."

Faith took a closer look at the vehicle that was in mint condition.

"Every guy's dream machine?" she guessed.

"You bet. Hop in and I'll take you home—you aren't dressed warmly enough to be out walkin'."

Faith told herself that she should decline the offer and use the bracing walk home to clear her head, to stick to what she'd told herself all day long—that even a faint kiss good-night was more than she should be doing with any man and that she needed to put things with Boone squarely and securely into a nothing-more-than-acquaintances box.

But she'd just spent the town meeting watching him and feeling dejected when she'd thought he might be ignoring her. Declining his offer wasn't what she was inclined to do, especially with the idea that he might have waited for her for just this reason rattling around in her head. Plus, Boone was right— she was freezing. And he was there. And he was Boone—charming, handsome…

Maybe I'll do better tomorrow, she told herself as she climbed into the passenger seat.

"I thought I'd just pop into the meeting tonight, do my part and leave," she explained as she closed the door. "I didn't expect to be going home this late."

"That'll teach you—nobody escapes town meetings early. So are you worn-out or can I interest you in a drive?"

She knew she should keep this to a quick and simple ride to her house. But now that she was in his car, with him, she couldn't make herself do that.

"If you have heat in this thing, I can probably spare some time," she said.

Boone grinned at her, turned a knob on the dashboard that sent warm air out of the vents and pulled away from the curb.

"How would you like to see what's been done to the north bridge now that you had to sit through the mayor talking about it?" Boone suggested. "Or have you already seen it?"

"I haven't seen it. But I'd like to," she said when she actually had more interest in things besides Northbridge's namesake.

But Boone took her at her word and headed out of town.

"What did you think of your government at work tonight?" he asked as he did.

Faith laughed. "I don't think I'll go again unless I have to."

"Yeah, I know. I wouldn't have been there, either, except I wanted to bring up the Hobbs' place."

"Couldn't you have just talked to your brother about it? Cam will probably be one of the cops checking it out now," Faith reasoned.

"I talked to him about it when I saw him earlier, but he didn't know if the place had been sold or rented. This was easier."

It seemed more complicated and time-consuming to her. But what did she know? Even if she could hope that he'd waited around to drive her home, she couldn't believe that he'd endured an entire boring town meeting for no other reason than to acciden-tally-on-purpose encounter her. And she certainly wasn't going to say any more about it and make it seem as if that was what she thought.

Instead, she seized his mention of where he'd been

before the meeting and said, "I forgot the last fittings on the suits for the groom and his groomsmen were tonight, weren't they? Was that where you saw your brother?"

"It was. Along with the rest of the male part of the wedding party and some highbrow suit-maker to the stars or something," Boone confirmed. "Wait'll you see us all—we're gonna be handsome devils."

Faith laughed at what she knew he thought was a joke. But she didn't need to be told that he—especially—would be a sight to behold in a custom-made suit, and she could hardly wait.

She didn't say that, though. She just changed the subject again, using his reference to the other groomsmen as a lead-in.

"You and all your brothers are groomsmen, right?"

"Right. And your cousin Noah is the best man."

"And you and Jon and Taylor are triplets—I'd forgotten that."

"What made you remember?"

"I came across Jon's and Taylor's graduation pictures in the yearbook beside yours. They looked a lot alike back then, but you hardly looked as if you were related to them."

"I was the runt of the litter—last one born, almost two full pounds smaller. My mom said Jon and Taylor starved me in the womb and that was why I pudged out as a kid—I was making up for it. Now we're all pretty much on the same level."

"Are the three of you closer to each other than to the rest of your siblings—the way twins can be?" she asked, wondering about him and what made him tick.

"Are we cliquish, do you mean? Nah. Not now and definitely not growing up. If anything we fought more with each other than with Cam or Scott or the girls because we shared a room."

"And it was a battleground?"

"Oh, yeah. I broke Jon's finger, Taylor broke my foot, Jon and I got together and shaved Taylor's head, Taylor and I duct-taped Jon to the closet door… My poor mother used to threaten to pad the walls. As it was, after my foot ended up in a cast, she took the headboards, bed frames and nightstands out of the room and just left us with mattresses on the floor so the walls and the floor were the only hard things we could bang into. And we still managed to do damage to each other—we all have scars with stories to go with them. And I can tell you from having my head held in it, that the reason dogs like to drink out of the toilet is that the water is really cold."

"Gross!" Faith exclaimed even as she laughed.

"It's okay," he assured. "I've washed since then."

They'd reached the bridge and Boone drove as close to it as he could get, letting his car lights shine in that direction so she could see it.

It was a covered bridge similar to several Faith had seen on trips to New Hampshire. Restoration had reinforced the stone piers that moored it to the banks of the stream it crossed. A steeply pointed black-shingled roof protected sides that were solid on the lower half and had crosshatch beams on the upper. It had been painted its original rustic red and rivaled the most beautiful of any of the bridges Faith had seen.

"The grounds are being worked on now," Boone told her. "The trees and bushes have all been trimmed and there's sod ordered. When it's finished, this whole area will be a park. The town's planning to divide some of the festivals so that not everything is held in the town square—some will be out here, particularly in the summer when the shade of the trees will cut the heat."

"I can't believe how good the bridge looks. I would have thought it was unsalvageable."

"It's been a big job but we're hoping to celebrate the completion sometime in June. Maybe if you're still around you can plan it."

Faith glanced from the bridge to Boone, who was looking only at her. "Is there an underlying message in that?" she asked with a smile she couldn't suppress.

He shrugged a careless shoulder. "I'm just sayin' that Northbridge could use a party-and-event-and-wedding planner. Something's always goin' on. So if you're thinking about staying, you could factor that in."

"I'll do that," she said offhandedly.

"That doesn't sound serious."

Faith was happy staring at him rather than at the bridge so she went on looking into that handsome face, but she didn't respond to his comment. Instead she said, "You just love it here, don't you?"

"Yep. It's in my blood."

"Did you miss it when you left for college?"

"Like crazy. Didn't you ever miss it?"

"A little. Here and there," she admitted. "But not like crazy."

He didn't seem to want to explore that because he changed the subject himself this time. "Are you gonna be able to pull off this flea market in one more day?"

"I think I am," Faith said.

He turned to brace his back against the door so he was facing her, propping a bent knee on the gear shift. It put his leg near enough to her thigh to set off a tiny buzz inside her, as if some kind of electrical charge actually passed between them.

"I've had an amazing amount of help," she continued, trying not to pay attention to that reaction. "It could never have been accomplished in New Haven, but with all the cooperation I've had it's come together. Tomorrow I'll run it like an emergency room. Donations will be accepted, sorted and then delivered to the areas that apply—a flea market triage."

"What kind of areas?"

"Clothes, kitchen gadgets, kids's stuff, furniture— for example. Oh, and we'll have a section for used farm equipment, saddles and things like that—there was a request for it and since there will also be the horse auction, that seemed to follow the theme. Anyway, I have volunteers working each area who will accept what's been sorted in triage. From there they'll tag everything and set it out on display. And even though it'll be a lot of work, I think by Saturday morning we'll be ready to go."

"You *are* good at this."

"Maybe you'd better wait and see if I make it," she suggested. "Did your receptionist tell you I called your office today and asked for photographs of the horses you're auctioning?"

Okay, and yes, she'd been hoping that the receptionist might put him on the phone and she'd get to talk to him…

"She did. I'll make sure you get them sometime tomorrow."

Would he bring them himself or send someone else? *It doesn't matter,* Faith told herself firmly.

"I want to put them on display in the gazebo first thing Saturday morning—well in advance of the auction. I'm hoping we'll draw an even bigger crowd of bidders that way. And you've arranged for the horses to all be at the town stables earlier in the day, right?"

"Right. Some of the ranchers from around here

have volunteered their time and their trailers to transport them. We should have them here by noon on Saturday, so anyone interested can look them over."

"And then the auction itself is at four o'clock, right? Luckily the mayor's brother-in-law is an auctioneer."

"What time do you have to get this all going tomorrow?" Boone asked then.

Faith grimaced at the thought. "I'm meeting my core team at the square at six."

"A.M.? And I'm keepin' you here tonight? Shame on me," he said with a wicked smile that seemed like a preview of the handsome devil he'd promised earlier. But then he said, "I suppose I should do what I signed on for and take you home, shouldn't I?"

She couldn't say that she was in no hurry because she liked sitting there with him, so she said, "You probably should."

He took a deep breath that made his chest raise gloriously and then exhaled to deflate it. "Too bad," he responded, echoing her sentiments when he'd told her the night before that he wouldn't lead her astray.

Then he turned to face the steering wheel again and put the still-running engine into reverse gear.

In order to see where he was going as he backed away from the bridge, he stretched a long arm across the top of her seat.

Faith suffered the strongest craving to have that

arm be around her instead and she held her own breath in order to fight it.

Nothing more than acquaintances, she reminded herself. *Just passing acquaintances...*

Once he'd reached a wider section of the road and could make a U-turn, he did that, removing his arm to drive. And that was when Faith breathed again.

"How's Charlie doing?" Boone asked as he headed back toward Northbridge proper.

"She's good," Faith said, seizing on the safety of small talk to help calm her unwanted responses to the man. "She likes the canned dog food. I haven't seen any signs that her mouth is bothering her, but she still won't listen to anything I say."

Boone shook his head and gave her a chastising look out of the corner of his eye. "She really has your number, Perry."

"Now when I get down on the floor to dominate her she just rolls over on her back, waits me out and then it's business as usual—she's into mischief, doing whatever she pleases and ignoring what I tell her."

Boone chuckled. "You *are* smarter than she is, you know."

"I'm not so sure."

"You need to be. You need to be convinced that you're the boss or she'll never buy it."

"Yeah, yeah, yeah," Faith muttered.

"What're you gonna do when you have kids? Let them walk all over you, too?"

He couldn't possibly know what a sore spot he'd just hit.

Except that it left her without a comeback for so long that he realized something was up because he said, "Uh-oh—I just stepped in something, didn't I?"

"No, it's okay," she lied. But it was feeble and he took his eyes off the road for a minute to let her know he knew it.

"I'm sorry," he said seriously.

"It's nothing," she insisted.

But it had been a conversation killer and they rode the rest of the way without saying much of anything.

Then there they were, parked in her driveway. And while Faith wanted to ask him in, she didn't do it.

But she also didn't rush out of the car and before she'd even thanked him for the ride he pivoted in his seat again to study her with eyes that were obviously curious about what nerve he'd touched.

"I'm sorry," he repeated. "I didn't know I was opening my big mouth about something I shouldn't."

"It's not a big deal."

She had the distinct impression that he knew she was still lying. But he didn't pry. He just went on staring at her so intently she could almost feel his gaze.

Then, just when she thought he was going to say more on the having-kids issue after all, he said,

"Wasn't it bad enough that you were light-years prettier than any girl in high school? Couldn't you have come back now all dumpy and frumpy and snaggle-toothed with warts on your nose?"

That made her laugh in spite of herself. And turn enough to look at him, to see for herself the improvements that time had made in him. In the ruggedly sculpted bounty of his face as those lake-water blue eyes bathed her in appreciation that fed her soul—something that she needed more than he could ever know....

"You got better but you wish I'd come back looking like a witch?" she challenged.

"That would be so great," he said with mock enthusiasm. "Is there anything you can do about it now?"

He was obviously trying to lighten the mood and make her feel better. And he was doing a good job because again she had to laugh at him. "You want me to snaggle my teeth and grow warts? I don't think so."

"It would make things a lot easier on me."

"What *things?*" she asked.

"Things like knowing I can't count on you being around forever so I should keep some space between us, and then picking you up on the street anyway and trying to interest you in a job," he confessed with a wry half smile.

So he was basically seesawing the same way she was.

And it seemed cruel, now that he'd told her that, to make him think she was above it, so she said, "I'm in the same boat. What do you think is going on with us?"

He shrugged again—one broad shoulder and one eyebrow, too. "Beats me. But it's makin' me a little nuts."

"Me, too," Faith whispered.

For a while they stared into each others' eyes as if there might be an answer there. But Faith didn't find one. All she found was a warmth that seemed to wrap around her as he reached a big hand to the side of her face, letting his palm follow the curve of her jaw.

He came away from the door then, urging her forward, too, until they met over the gear shift.

His eyes were still locked on hers, but not as if he were searching for clues now. Now he was looking at her as if he couldn't quite grasp the reality that she was there like that, with him.

Then he came in for a kiss that was different than the one he'd more or less stolen the night before. He came in with a slow deliberation, as if he wouldn't be rushed, as if tonight he wanted her forewarned and willing.

And she was.

She closed her eyes and just let it happen, just

let herself have that one moment when his lips covered hers.

They were soft at first, then only slightly more demanding, parted just enough, not too dry, not too moist. With a confidence that was so sexy, so alluring...

But it seemed as if it had only begun when he ended it and she had the sense that he was in the throes of that back-and-forth they'd just admitted to.

Faith didn't want to ask that, though, and find out that in the middle of kissing her he'd told himself he shouldn't be.

Instead she decided to make light of it. "So...*always?*" she said, referring to the comment he'd made the previous night about having always wanted to kiss her.

He smiled as if he knew exactly what she was talking about. "Maybe not *literally* always. But a dozen-plus years, anyway."

"No?" she said as if he were teasing her, still having trouble believing that he wasn't.

"Someday I might even tell you about it," he said with a grin. "But not today. You need to go in and get some sleep so you can get the flea market up and ready and make my cause a lot of money."

Faith gave herself another moment of looking at him, of wondering about that *always* business.

But she could see that he wasn't going to explain it now, no matter how long she waited. So she gave in.

"Thanks for the ride," she said.

His only response was to raise that beautifully chiseled chin in acknowledgment.

Then she got out of the car and went up to her front door, reasonably sure that he didn't come with her because if he had he would have kissed her again and he was wary of giving in to it.

But once her door was unlocked and she'd stepped into the warmth of her house she turned to see him still sitting there, watching her.

He's being careful, she thought. And it was what she should be, too.

But right then, no matter how smart she knew it was to practice caution, caution and being smart couldn't hold a candle to how much she wanted Boone to kiss her again.

And when he backed out of her driveway and she knew for a fact that wasn't going to happen, she couldn't help sighing a very deep and disappointed sigh as she closed her door.

Chapter Six

"Good timing! You just caught me," Faith said Friday afternoon when she answered her telephone at home and discovered it was her best friend from Connecticut calling.

"We've been playing phone tag all week. How can you be that busy in that Podunk town?" Nedra Carpenter demanded.

Nedra was right, they had been playing phone tag since Faith had called on Saturday night to let her friend know she'd arrived.

"From almost the minute I got here, I've been planning an impromptu benefit to raise money for a local horse rescue," Faith explained. "You just happened to call when I snuck away for a quick bathroom break—I have all of one day to get an entire flea market set up."

"You're working there? Already? I thought you were just going there to regroup and think things through? They can't have you, Faith! I won't give you up to them!"

Faith laughed. "Nobody *has* me, Ned. My sisters just rushed me into this thing. But I still haven't made any decision about here or there or anywhere or anything. I'm in flux."

"That's part of why I've been trying to talk to you this week—to give you a morsel that may tempt you in my direction."

"It's gotta be quick. I honestly shouldn't even have stolen these few minutes."

"It's *gotta* be quick?" Nedra echoed. "Oh my gawd, you sound like one of them already."

Faith laughed at her friend's mock-horror, but warned, "I'm telling you I only have a few minutes— spit it out or save it."

"Oh, that's not my Faith!" Nedra lamented before she got to the point. "I spent last weekend at the house party of none other than Franklin Hempstead."

Faith knew the significance of something like that even for Nedra, whose own family held a lofty standing in the social strata. The Hempsteads were more prominent than the Carpenters and Faith's former in-laws put together. They had more money, more power and more influence in higher places. An invitation to weekend with them was something her ex-husband had coveted.

"You've arrived!" Faith exclaimed over Nedra's coup.

"I know!" Nedra agreed, sounding as if she could hardly believe it herself. "It was last-minute and *all* thanks to you."

"How is it thanks to me?"

"You know that Franklin Hempstead has been living in Paris for the last year—"

"I know he was overseeing the loan of a part of his collection of Egyptian art to the Louvre, yes."

"Well, he just got back and heard about your divorce. And my impression was that since he couldn't track you down, he came after the next best thing— your closest friend. But only to talk about you."

"Why did he want to talk about me?"

"Don't be obtuse, Faith! You know the two of you have hit it off over the years working on all those art committees together."

"I wouldn't say we 'hit it off,'" Faith corrected.

"You've told me yourself that you always have a good time with him."

"He can be funny," Faith said simply.

"Yes, he said you share the same sense of humor. And love of the arts. And taste. And appreciation for—"

"I'm on the clock here, Ned," Faith cut her off before this dragged on for too long.

"Oh, fine," Nedra said impatiently. "The bottom line is that he was candid about his interest in you now that you're available." Nedra let only a brief dramatic pause fall before she added, "We're talking Franklin Hempstead! And while I know you don't care about his financial portfolio, he is nice-looking even if he isn't particularly tall. He's not at all full of himself, brilliant and exactly your type."

All of that was true.

"Plus," Nedra continued, "it would serve the Fosters right if you ended up a Hempstead! They'd die!"

That was true, too.

And while Faith hated to admit it, there was a tiny bit of satisfaction in that thought.

"So," Nedra went on, seeming oblivious to the fact that Faith hadn't made any response, "I told Franklin about my gallery opening and that you would be there and asked if he might like to come. You've never seen anyone jump at anything the way he jumped at that!"

Franklin Hempstead would be at the opening....

"Hello? Are you there? Have I lost the connection?" Nedra demanded.

"I'm here."

"What do you think?" Nedra asked, clearly expecting Faith to be as excited as she was by this news.

Faith understood the expectation. Nedra was right, Franklin Hempstead was exactly the kind of man Faith had been attracted to in the past—he had a masters degree from Oxford in art history, he was an opera and ballet enthusiast, he sat on the board of numerous museums and foundations for the arts, he saw every theater production worth seeing on Broadway, he was intelligent, well-spoken, witty, not at all arrogant or entitled despite his wealth and stature and, yes, he even had a sense of humor. Had she met him before meeting Shu Foster, had he shown the interest in her that he was showing now, she would have been as pleased as Nedra thought she should be and—if asked—wouldn't have hesitated a moment before accepting a date with him.

But now? Beyond feeling flattered and having that moment of rancorous satisfaction at the thought of how her ex and his family would feel, this just didn't do much for her.

Now what popped into her mind when she considered getting back into the dating pool was not Franklin Hempstead's face.

It was Boone Pratt's.

And *that* was beyond understanding…

"Faith? Are you there?" Nedra inquired a second time.

"I'm here," Faith repeated quietly.

"Well? What do you think? If Franklin Hempstead isn't enough to get you back here, nothing is!"

"You and your gallery opening are enough to get me back there," Faith assured.

"For a few days next week is all. I'm talking about more than that. Much more."

"I don't think I can make any decisions based on the fact that Franklin Hempstead asked about me," Faith reasoned.

"Will you at least stay longer than a few days next week because of it, though? I honestly think he'll invite you to cocktails. Or maybe even dinner. Or what if he's having another house party the next weekend? You'd want to go to that, wouldn't you? You'd stay for *that*...."

Faith had to admit that there was some appeal to what Nedra was assuming could happen. The same appeal that Connecticut and her old lifestyle and being with friends like Nedra had. A strong enough appeal that she hadn't sold her apartment and had left open the possibility of returning to it all.

On the other hand, that image of Boone kept inching into her mind, too, somehow dimming the allure.

"I can't say I *would* stay for any of that, no," she finally answered. "I mean, I might, if it felt right, but if it didn't, I wouldn't. I'd just have to see. But I really can't talk about it anymore. I have to go."

Nedra sighed elaborately enough for Faith to hear the huff. "Fine," her friend said again. "I'll be at the airport to pick you up Monday night, then."

"Quickly though—is everything going all right for the opening?"

"On schedule—you left such specific instructions for your old minion that it seems as if it will go off without a hitch."

Faith's *old minion* was the man she'd trained to take her job when she'd quit work to be married. For the opening of Nedra's gallery, Faith had done most of the planning before turning it over to him to actually put the wheels into motion while she packed up and moved.

"I'm glad everything is going the way it should be. I'm looking forward to it," Faith said. "But I have to run."

Nedra accepted that this time and they said their goodbyes.

It was only after Faith had hung up that it occurred to her that although she hadn't been lying when she'd told her friend that she was looking forward to Nedra's gallery opening, she wasn't looking forward to it quite as much as she had been before this last week.

This last week when Boone had come into the picture…

* * *

"Wow, you're like the poster child for worn-out."

Faith had seen Boone coming. His long legs and compact hips were encased in his ever-present jeans, his plain chambray shirt was tucked into them and, coming toward her on confident strides with just a hint of a swagger, he was a sexy sight for sore eyes.

"That's what every girl dreams of hearing," she countered the comment that had replaced a greeting.

It was after eight o'clock that evening and she and what was left of her volunteers were covering the last display area with sheets.

"But you'll be glad to know," she added, "that everything is up and ready to go first thing tomorrow morning. Unless, of course, vandals come in here tonight and tear it up or something."

"In Northbridge? Across the street from the cop shop? Nah."

"Your brother Cam did promise that the night shift would keep close tabs on it."

"Nobody will bother anything," Boone assured.

Faith paused to thank her volunteers for all their hard work and to tell them she'd see them tomorrow. Then she turned back to Boone. "Did you just come to make a crack about how bad I look?"

"Yep," he joked with a winning smile before he said, "The auctioneer got into town and wanted to see the horses so I took him out to the ranch. I just brought him back and I was on my way to the old homestead to pick up my suit for the wedding when I saw you still out here. Thought I'd stop."

He surveyed the sea of sheets, tarps and blankets that dotted the square to protect the items to be sold and then said, "Lot of stuff. Lot of work."

"I think every basement, cellar, crawlspace, closet and garage in this town got emptied out for this. There's more than I ever imagined there would be. Which is good, because if I'd had any idea how much we'd be dealing with I would never have tried to do this in such a rush."

"But now you've made it."

"This far, anyway. Tomorrow is another day."

Boone stopped looking at the setup for the flea market and turned his focus solely on her. "Have you eaten?"

"I've had two containers of yogurt and half of a doughnut since I got up this morning."

"I've done better than that, but I haven't had dinner yet. How 'bout I treat?"

Faith didn't know whether she was more tired or hungry. But what she did know was that after an extremely full day outside, handling the dusty donations of the entire town, she was in no shape to go to a restaurant.

"I'd take you up on that but I'm too much of a mess—the poster child for worn-out needs a shower."

"Pizza, then," he persisted. "You go home, shower and get comfortable, I'll pick up my suit, order the pizza and bring it over."

The usual shouldn'ts raced into her mind, but as with every other time she was faced with a chance to spend time with Boone, *wanting* to be with him was the stronger drive. And Faith was just too exhausted to fight that stronger drive.

So she didn't try. "That sounds fabulous."

"Can you get home on your own?" he asked.

Faith laughed. "I *must* look bad." Then she nodded toward Main Street. "I drove over to bring my own contributions to the sale. I think I can drive back."

"I'm parked down South Street. I'll meet you at your place in—what?—half an hour?"

"I'd like longer than that but I'll hurry. I'll also leave the front door unlocked in case you get there before I'm presentable—just come in. Charlie will bark her head off to announce you, I'm sure, but if she doesn't, yell for me and I'll be out as soon as I can."

"Okay. What do you like on your pizza?"

"Meat!" she said like a deranged cavewoman. "Sausage and pepperoni. And mushrooms and black olives and green peppers and—"

"Loaded—I get the idea. I'll take care of it," he said with a smile fit to bask in.

She didn't have much of a chance, though, because with the details decided, he headed off in the direction from which he'd come.

Rewarding herself for a long day's work, Faith stole a glance at how great his rear end looked in those jeans. And oh, did it look great!

Then she turned towards Main Street and her own car.

As she did it struck her that she couldn't envision Franklin Hempstead involved in the sort of evening she'd just planned with Boone.

And yet she was surprised to realize that exhausted or not, she was more eager to share a pizza with the cowboy than she had been for anything Nedra thought could be in the offing with the other man.

The man who was the embodiment of what she'd always thought she wanted...

"I brought you a present."

"Besides the pizza I just ate like a glutton?" Faith asked.

It was approaching ten o'clock. After her shower and a quick shampoo, she'd slipped into a light-weight cashmere sweatsuit with a hoodie top. She'd blown her hair dry, curled the ends over a round brush and left it loose, but as far as makeup was concerned, she'd only had to apply mascara because being out in the April sunshine had added enough rose to her cheeks to keep her from needing blush.

Boone had arrived just as she was breaking out the mascara. He'd quieted Charlie in record time and had been in the kitchen setting the table when Faith came out. They'd eaten, then moved into the living room where Faith had collapsed at one end of the leather sofa and Boone had taken the other end. She hadn't seen any sign of a present.

Boone spread his knees wide apart, bending over to reach under the couch. He pulled a white box tied with a red ribbon from what was apparently his hiding place, but Faith was stuck more on the sight of those thick, widespread thighs and the instant image of having them straddling her.

She blinked away the mental blip that had distracted her fatigued brain and forced her focus on the gift.

"Charlie must not have seen you hide that there or she would have dragged it out—she loves to unwrap packages," Faith said with a glance at her schnauzer who had, indeed, perked up and come to see what was going on.

"She saw. I just told her to leave it alone."

"And that worked?"

"She left it alone, didn't she?"

There was no arguing that.

"She thinks it's hers now," Faith said.

"Well, she's wrong," Boone declared, handing it

to Faith. "It's yours. For doing everything you're doing for the horse rescue."

"You didn't have to—"

"It's a little for me, too," he said slyly.

Faith accepted the package, pulling a free end of the ribbon to offer to Charlie. Charlie grasped it in her mouth, gave a growl, shook her head back and forth furiously and then tugged until she'd successfully freed it from the box to run with it like a prize of war.

Then Faith lifted the lid on the box. Inside was a pair of blue jeans.

She laughed and rolled her eyes. "You can't get over my clothes, can you?"

"Just tryin' to bring you back into the fold."

"Thank you, *Reverend Pratt*. But obviously your *fold* is different than my grandfather's, because he frowned on his granddaughters wearing jeans," she said as she took them out. "How did you know what size?"

"Eve helped. Before she came to work on the flea market with you today—and during my lunch break—she met me. Now you can ditch those jean-impersonators you had on the other night and get back into the real thing. I'll bet you haven't worn them since you were in high school."

"And is that the part that's for you—seeing me in what I wore in high school? A *dozen-plus* years ago?"

"The part that's for me is not having to see you in

jeans that somebody's stuffy mother would wear," he said, giving as good as he got.

"Well, thank you, anyway. I think," she said, setting the gift on the coffee table.

Once she had, she pivoted to sit with her back against the sofa arm, putting her feet flat on the cushion and hugging her shins so she could look at him as she weighed whether or not to pry into what she wanted to pry into.

Her curiosity over the things he'd alluded to about their high school days had niggled at her even in the midst of all she'd been doing for the flea market. Tonight she was just tired enough and just slap-happy enough to consider pushing for some satisfaction to that curiosity now that the subject had again been introduced.

Should I or shouldn't I...?

Settling in himself, Boone angled in her direction. He stretched a substantial arm along the top of the back pillow, resting one of those massive thighs on the couch and covering her bare feet with his calf in a way that shouldn't have had any effect on her and yet sent goose bumps up her legs.

"So I want to know," she said, deciding that it was better to pry than to think too much about those goose bumps or what was causing them.

"What?" he asked.

"First you were mad at me over something I

said in high school. Then there was the *always* business that dates back to that, too. And now you want me dressed the way I did then. What's up with all of that?"

He shrugged. "You've found me out—you were the first girl I ever noticed. I had a *huge* crush on you."

"You did not," Faith refuted because not only did she find that impossible to believe, his tone was extremely facetious.

"I did," he insisted but not enough that it convinced her.

"If you had, I would have known."

"How would you have known if I didn't tell anybody?"

"You would have told someone. If you had a *huge* crush you wouldn't have been able to keep it a secret from your friends or your brothers."

"Sure I would have. Secrets aren't that hard to keep. Particularly when you know that if it got out you'd never live it down. The fat, baby-faced, backward kid having it bad for you? No way I would have let *that* get around."

"I'm not buying this. You never even said two words to me," Faith said, thinking he was pulling her leg. "If you had had a thing for me you would have hung around me, you would have talked to me."

"Maybe I was The Invisible Admirer," he said as if it were the name of a comic book superhero. "And remember, I did hang around close enough to hear all your get-out-of-Northbridge stuff."

It sounded like a lie peppered with just enough plausibility to leave her wondering.

"Really? You had a crush on *me?*" she said dubiously once more.

"Not just a crush," he corrected. "A *huge* crush. So when you were going around telling your friends how much you wanted out of here, how could I *not* take it personally? To me, *I* was the hayseed you couldn't wait to get away from."

Okay, so that sounded genuine. Sort of. If he hadn't said it with such a melodramatic tone.

"If you're serious, I'm sorry," she said, calling his bluff.

"You should be sorry," he countered as if she'd injured him terribly.

"So, did you stalk me?" she asked, testing what still seemed not quite true.

"Detours past your house, timing things so I was near your locker between classes, waiting around so we left school at the same time—does that count as stalking?"

"I don't know about stalking, but it does seem like what a teenage boy with a crush would do," she said. "But how is that I never noticed any of it?"

"I was The Invisible Admirer," he repeated.

"I suppose Northbridge is so small that your being

around wouldn't have seemed like anything out of the ordinary," she said, still trying to sort out whether he was answering honestly or not.

"Or I missed my calling and should have been an undercover operative," he said with a wiggle of his eyebrows.

"You didn't do anything creepy, did you? Like peek in my windows?"

"Your bedroom was on the second floor—how would I have done that?"

So he'd paid enough attention to know which room in her parents' house was hers. Or maybe he'd just learned that somewhere along the way and was using it to his advantage now.

Then he added, "I leaned against the big tree across the street from your house and stared up at the light I could see through the curtains, mooning over what I wanted and couldn't have, my heart breaking...."

More melodrama.

"That's either really sad or you're making all this up," she said, the theatrics putting doubt in her mind again. "Or maybe—because you know I like the theater—you're just doing a private performance for me here tonight. Is that it?"

He shook his head morosely, like a bad actor not breaking character. "I'm not making it up. You were my dream girl. And it was demoralizing to know my dream girl thought I was a loser."

"I didn't think you were a loser."

"Because you didn't think of me at all."

Faith studied him, still unsure. "You're just putting me on, aren't you?"

Boone gave a Cheshire-cat smile and cocked one eyebrow at her, leaving her guessing.

Was he getting some sort of satisfaction out of that?

"I think you're just having fun at my expense," she said, enjoying this less than when it began. "I'll bet you'd barely reached puberty in high school and didn't know or care that any girl existed—especially me—until you heard me say something that insulted you. Then you didn't like me at all and now you're getting even by pretending you had a crush on me."

"How would that be *getting even?*"

She didn't want to admit that it felt good to think that she might have been special to him. So she just said, "I don't know. I just know that I hope you're not making this up, but I think you are."

Boone's Cheshire-cat smile broadened into a grin. He didn't tell her whether she was right or wrong, though, and it tweaked something more than curiosity in her suddenly.

"Fine," she said then, knowing she was echoing Nedra. "You wouldn't be the first man to take me for a sucker."

The grin disappeared and was replaced by a

frown. "I don't know what that means but it isn't something I'd ever do to you."

"No? Maybe you're trying to see just how dumb and gullible I am and in the end the joke is going to be on me—why else wouldn't you just say straight-out *Hey, I had a crush on you in high school?*"

"Hey, I had a crush on you in high school," he repeated by rote.

"Too late," she accused angrily. "It's not sweet or touching or nice now. It's ruined."

He stared at her from beneath that beetled brow. Then, as if she'd touched a raw nerve in him, he said, "How far out on the limb do you want me?"

"How are you going out on a limb?" she demanded.

He shrugged but didn't explain.

"It's just important for people to be up front with me. I don't like being played," she told him.

"I guess so if this set you off so much. I thought we were just having some fun."

"So it *was* a joke."

Boone's eyebrows arched and he drew back slightly, as if he wasn't quite sure what was going on, and that was when it struck Faith that maybe this had all been more important to her than it should have been.

But somewhere along the way it had become bigger than the idea that he might or might not have had a teenage infatuation with her. It had become about her falling for something that was smoke and mirrors.

"Jokes aren't funny when someone is the brunt of them," she muttered.

Boone still studied her, clearly confused by how far this had gone. Then, without any caginess, he said, "I don't know why it matters to you now, but I wasn't joking. It was all true."

"Then why did you make it sound like it might not be?"

He shrugged again, this time as if he wasn't sure why he'd done that. "To retain a shred of dignity?"

That hadn't occurred to her. She'd been too lost in her own baggage. And now she saw that she'd made something that was apparently difficult for him to admit even harder. No wonder things had tensed between them.

Faith thought that since she'd done her part in causing the tension, she should help reduce it if she could. So she said, "I really am sorry if it was awful for you to like me when we were teenagers."

"It's part of adolescence," he said.

"Then maybe I shouldn't have pushed it now. Although I don't know why you thought telling me was undignified or going out on a limb."

He shrugged a third time, once more not explaining and instead saying, "Who knows, maybe my secret crush on you made me the man I am today."

"Then it was worth it," she said somewhat under her breath.

It took him a moment but then he smiled a little, leaned forward and clasped his hands around her ankles. He pulled her toward him at the same time he moved toward her.

"While we're at it I might as well tell you one other thing," he said when they were nearly nose-to-nose in the center of the leather sofa, her rear end butted against his thigh and her feet on the other side of him. "I like you now, too."

"And it's driving you nuts because you wish you didn't," she reminded him of what he'd said the night before.

His grin grew wider. "That's not exactly what I said, but as I recall you were right in there with me," he pointed out.

Faith didn't deny it. But she did go out on a small limb of her own and say, "I'm sorry for whatever you went through. But for me, right now, it goes a long way to hear that *I* was the dream girl."

The frown he shot at her was curious but before he could say anything, she said, "Don't ask."

"I guess you'll tell me when you slip up and your mouth gets ahead of your brain like mine did tonight, huh?" he said instead.

"Maybe," she allowed. "Is that how the crush confession happened—it was a slip?"

"I definitely didn't have plans to tell you. Then it started coming out and…" Yet another shrug. "It's probably better if we just leave it alone."

Faith nodded and decided she owed him a little something for the emotions and reactions she hadn't been able to control tonight either. "You know, I like you now, too."

He smiled again, showing her those heartbreaker dimples that creased his cheeks. "Good. You had me a little worried there for a while—gettin' all prickly."

"Prickly?" she said, taking issue.

He challenged her to deny it with another raised eyebrow. But he also looked into her face, into her eyes for a moment before he smiled even bigger and said, "Did we just have a fight?"

"Maybe," Faith allowed. "A small one."

"You know what that means…."

"That we stumbled into a problem area and worked it out?"

He shook his head. "That we have to make up."

"Ah. We *have* to?"

"It's a law," he decreed right before he leaned in slightly farther and kissed her.

She didn't know exactly when that kiss moved from a make-up kiss to something deeper, but it did. Maybe it was when his mouth opened wider or when hers did, too. Maybe it was when his tongue came to trace a tickling tip along the scant inner edge of her lips. Or when it found a clear path in to meet and greet her tongue. But whenever or however it happened, that kiss took on a life of its own and drew her in.

One of his arms came around her, pulling her in close enough so that her breasts brushed his chest and she discovered her nipples were standing high and hard. His other hand cupped the side of her face, doing a sensual massage that lulled her even as her tongue answered the call of his. Circles and strokes and tip-to-tip, they toyed with each other, mouths wider still.

Faith raised her own hands to Boone's chest and, even though it looked solid through his clothes, she was shocked by the power and mass of the hidden muscles. She was left shocked and impressed and intrigued, and wondering how it would feel bare.

But she couldn't venture that far, and so, thinking that she was avoiding temptation, she slipped her arms around him.

It was a miscalculation because the feel of his back was every bit as good. Muscles bulged there, too, rippling and rolling beneath her touch and making her want just as badly to feel them with her naked palms.

The only thing that helped was that his other arm slid from her face to her back, and with both of his arms around her, too, he was holding her in a way that felt so good she didn't want to do anything that would disturb it.

Boone took that kiss to yet another level, pressing her head back and plundering her mouth in delicious domination.

Civilized, mechanical, perfunctory—that was how she'd been kissed for the last six years. And before Shu Foster, even the best kisses hadn't been anything at all like this one! In fact, never in her life had she been kissed the way Boone was kissing her and she was slightly surprised that she could keep up.

But apparently kissing was instinctive. Faith kissed him back with just as much abandon, just as much fervor and gusto as he was giving her. With her mouth as seeking as his, with her tongue as bold as his, with hands that caressed and massaged and pressed into him every bit as much as his caressed and massaged and pressed into her. If kisses could be art, then she recognized a masterpiece when she experienced one and she just wanted it to go on and on until she couldn't be kissed anymore....

Except that just as she was thinking that, Boone robbed her of his mouth.

She opened her eyes to a look of hunger on his handsome face before he hid it from her and merely arched his eyebrows as if he were just waking from a trance. Then he dropped his chin to the top of her head and said, "Okay, I'm all made up. How about you?"

The words were glib, but the deep, ragged tone in his voice gave away what that kiss had done to him, too.

And as Faith felt the heat of him bathing her face, as she breathed in the spring-rain scent of his cologne, as she fought the urge to poke the tip of her tongue out to touch to his Adam's apple, she wondered fleetingly if saying that she wasn't quite made up yet would get her kissed like that again.

But by then a hint of reason had nudged into her consciousness and she knew another kiss like that would have her lost for good. So she tried to sound less shaken than she actually was and said, "All made up," but in a voice that came out barely above a breathy whisper.

Boone took his chin from the top of her head, pulled his arms from around her and sat up straight enough to separate them.

Reluctantly, Faith retrieved her arms from around him, too, folding them primly in the V of her lap.

"I should go so you can get some rest before tomorrow," Boone said then, placing his hands on her cashmere-clad knees and squeezing them.

What instantly sprang to Faith's mind was the image of having those hands on her breasts instead, and, like with the earlier flash of massive thighs straddling her, she knew she had to stop thinking like that in a hurry.

She lifted her legs, swiveled and put her feet on the

floor. "You have office hours in the morning, don't you?" she asked, finding refuge in a safe subject.

"I do, but I only accepted appointments until ten," he confirmed as he stood. "Then I'll be at the stables so I can answer questions about the horses before they go on the auction block."

"So you'll have a busy day, too."

"Seems like I will."

Faith stood and followed him to the front door. "Thanks for the pizza and the jeans," she said.

"If you can't stand 'em you don't have to wear 'em," he told her as he reached for the door handle.

"And go around looking like somebody's stuffy mother?" she countered.

He smiled and, without even knowing she was going to do it, when the creases appeared in his cheeks, she drew an index finger down one of them.

She snatched her hand away when she realized what she'd done, but by then Boone had reached a hand to her hip in what seemed almost like reflex.

He spent a moment peering down into her eyes again before using that single hand to pull her forward enough to kiss her again, a kiss much like the one the night before and nowhere near as powerful as what they'd shared on the couch.

Then he said, "See you tomorrow."

"See you tomorrow," Faith echoed as he let go of her and left.

A tiny whimper sounded from far below her as Boone closed the door behind him.

Faith looked down, realizing only then that Charlie had tagged along with them to the door.

"What was that for? Don't you want him to go?" she asked her pet.

Charlie whimpered again then let out a yip that secmed like confirmation.

"And he didn't even kiss you until you turned to mush inside," Faith whispered to her dog, tempted to whimper right alongside Charlie for just one more kiss like she didn't know kisses could be....

Chapter Seven

The flea market on Saturday was a roaring success. The spring weather was warm and sunny, so not only did everyone in Northbridge come out, but people drove in from neighboring towns and even from Billings.

Overseeing it all, Faith ran around nonstop the entire day. And although she kept an eye out for Boone, she assumed he must have been equally as busy at the stables after his office closed because she didn't see him until long after word had spread to her that the auction had concluded.

She and the last of the volunteers were dismantling the display areas by then and when she looked up he was headed toward her.

But before he reached her, he was intercepted by a group of men dressed in Western suits and cowboy hats.

It was a loud group and even from a distance Faith heard them insisting on buying Boone a drink. He tried to get out of it, but ultimately all he managed was a wave to her as he was swept out of the town square and up Main Street.

He never reappeared and by the time the square was back to its normal state and everyone had been thanked and sent home, Faith merely went home, too, resigned to the fact that this was going to be a basically Boone-less day.

She told herself as she showered when she got home at nearly nine o'clock that she had no business feeling as disappointed as she did. That it should not be factoring into her mood. That it was good for her to go a day—or a week or a month or forever—not having contact with him. That there was no reason for her to have contact with him since there was nothing between them.

Except that kiss the night before that had opened her eyes.

But still, she lectured herself firmly, with Charlie's tooth problems behind her and the flea market over, it was time for her to do what she'd come to Northbridge to do—get her life and her head straightened out so she could make some decisions about her future.

And that future didn't involve Boone Pratt.

Which meant that this was the perfect time for him to stop being a part of things the way he had been since she'd come back.

And yet, when her doorbell rang only minutes after she'd gotten out of the shower and dressed for bed, the mere possibility that it might be him made her want to jump for joy.

Wishing her hair wasn't wet and pulled into a rubber band at her crown, and that she had on some mascara, she nevertheless ran to the door rather than risk him leaving.

Charlie was doing her usual frantic barking in response to the bell and Faith's attempts to shush her didn't do the trick, so Faith ignored her pet and opened the door. Probably with more enthusiasm than was called for, but she just couldn't help it.

Charlie went instantly silent when the schnauzer saw that their visitor was indeed Boone. Faith told herself that one glimpse of him should not have been all it took for everything to seem right with the world. But that was how it was anyway.

So she said, "Hi," and tried not to smile too big.

"What are your feelings about hoagie sandwiches? Because I make a spectacular one and if you didn't have time to stop and eat yesterday I can't believe you did today. I know I didn't, and I didn't think you'd want pizza again, so I got all this stuff—" he paused to peer into the paper bag he was carrying in one arm and then looked at her again "—and I'm too hungry to take it home before I get to eat it and I thought I might be able to persuade you to let me use your kitchen to put it together and then I'd share it with you."

"That was a mouthful," Faith said.

"So's this. What do you say?"

"I'm starving again and too tired to fix anything myself so I was going to eat cereal. Your sandwich sounds better," she said, pretending that she was just glad for the food as she and Charlie stepped aside.

"Can I have a few minutes to dry my hair first?" she asked as Boone came in. "I just got out of the shower."

"Sure," he allowed, bending over to pet the waiting dog. "Charlie and I will be in the kitchen."

Boone headed there and Charlie followed as if she belonged to *him*.

Then Faith made a mad dash to her bathroom where she took her hair out of the rubber band and blew it dry so that it would fall freely around her shoulders. Once that was accomplished, she brushed on mascara and debated changing her clothes.

Thinking that she'd be alone for the remainder of the evening, she'd dressed in a pair of navy-blue knit pajama pants and a matching cap-sleeved

T-shirt that fit her like a second skin. And she hadn't put on a bra.

But if she changed, Boone was bound to notice. And he always made such a big deal about her overdoing the clothes she wore that she knew putting on something better now would provoke more of that.

She should at least add a bra, though, she told herself.

Except that she was tired. And comfortable.

And it was warm in the house, she rationalized. And she wasn't all that well-endowed. And the T-shirt was a dark color and tight enough to have a sort of compression effect all on its own. So couldn't she forgo a bra just this once?

She knew she shouldn't.

But she decided to anyway.

Boone was standing at her kitchen counter with Charlie sitting at his feet when she joined them. She gave Boone a quick once-over and realized for the first time that he wasn't dressed the way he had been when she'd seen him for that brief moment at the town square earlier. The jeans he had on now were more worn-out. Instead of a dress shirt, he was now wearing a plain white crew-neck T-shirt with short sleeves that were stretched tight around impressive biceps. And not only was he freshly shaven and smelling of that cologne she liked so much, his hair was also damp. Obviously he'd showered before stopping by.

"What can I do to help?"

"I don't need any help. Go sit down, relax and open your mail," he answered with a nod at the overnight-mail envelope that she'd brought in with her when she'd arrived home and left on the kitchen table.

"You don't want me to do *anything?*" she persisted.

"You can pour us both a glass of that wine I brought. I already opened it."

"I saw you get kidnapped by those men in the square," she said as she got out two glasses. "I thought you'd be off drinking most of the night to celebrate selling all the horses and doing as well as we did with the flea market."

"*Those men* are members of the Cattlemen's Association. They came in from Missoula for the auction. I couldn't turn them down. But I begged off as soon as I could."

Faith wondered if he'd *begged off* because he hadn't wanted to spend tonight drinking with the other men or because he'd planned on coming over.

Then he said, "If I was going to celebrate what was accomplished today it wouldn't have been with those guys, anyway. Two of them pooled their resources and bought one of the horses, but they still didn't do as much as you did."

That embarrassed her slightly—especially when it came with a look of appreciation for things other than horse rescue.

"Is this a celebratory sandwich?" she joked with a nod toward his handiwork.

"Nah, you deserve more than this. I'll have to think of a better reward for all your hard work."

"I thought the jeans you brought last night were my reward," she reminded.

"Which you didn't wear today," he pointed out.

"I thought I needed a more professional look. I'll get to them, don't worry."

His gaze dropped to what she had on and he gave a wicked smile. "This is good, too," he said in a gravelly voice that made her think twice about having left a bra behind. Particularly when she felt her nipples harden for no reason.

It was too late to go back for the bra, but she couldn't stay where she was, either, so she finally poured the Shiraz and took her glass to the table.

The express-mail envelope was from Nedra and she told him that—and who Nedra was—as she tore it open, pretending all the while to ignore her body's reaction to him.

"I don't know why Nedra is sending me anything. I'll see her on Monday."

"Is she coming here?" Boone asked.

"No," Faith answered, going on to tell him that

she was returning to Connecticut for Nedra's gallery opening.

"It's only for a couple of days, then?" he asked as if it mattered to him.

"Or maybe a week…"

Faith reached into the envelope and pulled out pictures of Franklin Hempstead from the house party Nedra had attended the weekend before. There was also a full sheet of Nedra's stationery and THIS IS WHAT YOU'RE MISSING printed in large block letters.

"Who's he?"

Boone had finished making the sandwich and used the cutting board to bring it to the table. He apparently had no compunction about peering at the photographs that Faith was wishing weren't out in the open as he set down the wooden board and Charlie took up a spot between their chairs.

"This is a man named Franklin Hempstead," Faith said, deciding there was no cause to be mysterious.

"Franklin, huh? Not Frank?"

"No, Franklin."

"Who's *Franklin?*"

"He's just someone I know—we've worked on a lot of committees together. Nedra is trying to get me to decide to live in Connecticut, the same way my sisters are trying to get me to stay here, and Nedra thinks Franklin is bait."

"Is he?"

Just *how* honest was she going to be?

Faith shrugged. "We've seemed to have a lot in common in the past, but I don't really know him outside of committee work—it isn't as if that's enough to base a decision on." Even if it did feel good to know Franklin Hempstead was interested…

Boone picked up one of the photos and gave it a thorough study. "This is how I've pictured your ex-husband in my mind the past few days—the hair, the clothes, I'll bet his nails are manicured—things that scream uppercrust."

"I don't know why you've been picturing my ex-husband at all, but there are some similarities," Faith admitted.

"This one's a moneybags, too?"

Faith laughed. "I don't think he'd like being called that, but yes, he's a moneybags, too. More so, even, than my former husband. In fact, Franklin Hempstead is someone who could elevate my ex-husband's standing with nothing but a nod in his direction."

"So you could really stick it to the ex by hooking up with this guy."

Faith understood why Nedra was taking this path but why was Boone?

"I could," she agreed. "But that isn't any reason to *hook up* with anyone, is it?"

Boone mimicked her shrug. "Not for me, but I don't know what the high-and-mighty do."

Faith groaned at that remark. "I should pick up your fancy sandwich and use it as a baseball bat and hit you for saying that again," she threatened. Only not in anger, because it suddenly occurred to her that Boone might actually be jealous. And she loved that idea.

"Are we gonna have another fight?" he asked.

Making up *had* been worth it....

"Because," he continued, "I just opened your refrigerator to see if you had any mayonnaise and if you use this sandwich to hit me, you'll ruin it and there's nothing around here to replace it with. Unless you count yogurt, pudding and cookie dough, and nobody can live on those."

"Maybe the high-and-mighty can," she countered facetiously. "That and all the leftover Chinese food I've been eating for breakfast."

He didn't say anything in response. Instead he focused on cutting the loaf of French bread that he'd slit in half, filled with meats and cheeses, lettuce, tomatoes, olives and artichoke hearts, and then put back together.

Faith had the sense that he was using the task to deal with whatever the snapshots had provoked in him, and she decided to aid the cause by putting them back in the envelope. Then she set the envelope on the counter behind her.

"The pictures were just Nedra thinking she was being funny," she said in an attempt to make less of it.

Boone served her a section of the sandwich, took one for himself and gave Charlie a slice of tomato, obviously not appreciating her friend's humor.

After they'd both tasted the sandwich and Faith had given him well-deserved accolades for it, Boone took a drink of his wine, leveled his blue eyes on her and said, "You know, over the years I've turned a deaf ear to most everything that was said about you."

"Was I the talk of the town?"

"No more than anyone else. It was just the usual stuff. Folks would ask Eve how you and Eden were doing, if you were still living in Connecticut, if Eden was still in Hawaii, what the two of you were up to—that kind of thing."

"But you had such a grudge against me that you didn't want to know what I was doing so you didn't listen to any of it."

"Pretty much, yeah. I heard that you snagged yourself some blue-blooded husband. I heard that it didn't work out. But beyond that—nothin'. And now I'm wishing I'd paid more attention."

"Why is that?"

"Because now I *want* to know what went on with you and all I've been gettin' are crumbs that make me wonder even more."

"Crumbs?"

"Last night you said I wouldn't be the first one to take you for a sucker," he said. "You made a big deal out of how important it is for people to be up front with you. The night before that you shut down when I just mentioned having kids. Jared said you were the sacrificial lamb—" He cut himself short.

But Faith wasn't going to let him off the hook. "My cousin said I was a sacrificial lamb?"

Obviously he knew he'd been caught.

Boone took a resigned breath, sighed it out and confessed. "I asked Jared a few things when we were having the suit-fittings, thinking that maybe the two of you were close since you were both in the same area of the country after leavin' here. But he didn't give me anything to go on, either, except to say that you made your in-laws look good and they turned around and made you their sacrificial lamb—whatever that meant."

Faith was reasonably sure where this was going and she took another bite of sandwich while she considered whether or not to stop it before it got there.

She hadn't been willing to tell Boone about her past before this, but they'd come a long way and tonight—after accidentally throwing another man in his face when all he'd done was come to make her dinner—she thought maybe he deserved something in return.

She finished her bite, drank some wine, and said, "What do you want to know?"

"Everything. Start with the ex's name—I don't think I even know that for sure."

"Shu—as in Shubert—"

"*Shubert? Franklin* instead of Frank? Do any of these guys have regular names?"

"Like *Boone?*" she said, teasing him. "Shu was named for his great-grandfather."

"And where'd you meet *Shubert?*"

"It was about six years ago. I was only a few months out of college with a business degree and working for an event planner in New York. Shu's parents hired us to go to Connecticut to plan the renewal of their wedding vows for their thirtieth anniversary. I met Shu when I was doing that."

"Love at first sight?"

"We dated for six months—he stayed in a penthouse the family had in New York just so he could go on seeing me when I'd finished the party for his parents. Then he proposed."

"And he was Prince Charming?"

"He was, actually. He was everything I was sure I wanted in a man—debonair, polite, smart, personable. He took me to the opera and the ballet, to plays, to museums. There was tennis and golf and dancing at his country club. He was sophisticated and cosmopolitan and he swept me off my feet."

Faith paused and stared at Boone pointedly. "And no, I didn't care that he had money. I would have thought he was just as perfect for me even if he hadn't had a stock portfolio that took legions of brokers to keep up with. He could have been an average nine-to-fiver who just—"

"Knew and loved all that artsy-fartsy stuff and wasn't from Northbridge," Boone finished for her.

"Yes," she said because it was true.

"So *in spite* of the money he was Mr. Right."

"That's what I thought. Which is why, when he proposed, I said yes, and after nine months of planning the wedding his mother wanted us to have, we were married," Faith said, putting the rest into a nutshell.

"Not the wedding *you* wanted, the wedding his mother wanted?"

"I was not exactly a match made in heaven in his parents' opinion—to them, Shu was marrying beneath him. But for reasons I only learned much later, they had to settle for me. My mother-in-law said the right kind of wedding would help me be accepted in their social circle since I wasn't really *one of them*."

"And you took that?" Boone asked in outrage.

"I loved Shu. I thought he was everything I'd ever wanted. He knew his mother was a pain but he convinced me to just humor her, so I did. Besides, even though I knew how to put on the best society parties and weddings and charity balls, I didn't know anything about being *one of them*. I figured I needed some grooming and guidance or I might embarrass Shu, and I didn't want that to happen."

"You thought of yourself as a hayseed from a hick small town."

Faith shrugged again to concede that.

"So you had the wedding your mother-in-law wanted you to have…"

"It *was* a beautiful wedding. Beatrice had taste, I'll give her that."

"And then what?"

"Then I thought I was happily married. For three and a half years. Sure, Shu was away a lot on business—the family fortunes were in different businesses and investments and corporations all over the country and he said it just went with the territory and I didn't have any reason to doubt that. And when he was home he was a really good husband—attentive, interested, loving…"

Her voice cracked over that part and she sipped her wine as the memory of perfunctory affection flashed through her mind. Perfunctory affection that she'd tried—and failed—to heat up, that had eventually made her think that maybe she wasn't attractive or sexy enough, that had made her wonder if she'd traded a fulfilling love life for culture.

One thing was for sure, Shu Foster had never kissed her the way Boone had kissed her the night before….

"You said something a while back about living

with his family?" Boone prompted, probably because she'd stalled and he wanted to get her started again.

"We had our own section of the family home," Faith said. "Bedroom, bathroom, sitting room—not a kitchen or anything, but basically a private living area. Initially Shu promised it was a temporary arrangement until we built a house. But every time I tried to get that started he'd balk. Then he said since he would inherit that house eventually anyway, why should we build something else."

"But he wanted a place separate from your family here, in Northbridge. That's why you bought this place," Boone said, referring to what she'd told him about her house.

"He didn't really want to associate with my family at all," Faith said, unable to keep a hint of bitterness out of her voice. "Besides, sending me to visit my family alone gave him whole blocks of free time."

They'd both finished their sandwiches by then and Boone had settled back in his chair, one arm over the back of it, one resting on the table with his big hand around the stem of the wineglass. His focus was totally on Faith, who was clasping her glass with both hands in a white-knuckled grip as she told him things she wished she could forget about.

"Okay, so you were happily married for three and a half years," Boone said to spur her on.

"After three years I wanted to start a family. Shu seemed to barely be listening when I brought it up—as if I were talking about changing the drapes. But he agreed and I went off of birth control. When nothing happened after six months—except that he bought me Charlie—I thought we should see a doctor just for general checkups to make sure there wasn't anything keeping us from conceiving. But while Shu hadn't seemed to care about having a baby, he had very strong opinions about seeing a doctor—there was no way. He said that having kids would either happen or it wouldn't and that was as far as he was going. I was frustrated and upset and I vented a lot of it—to Nedra, to other friends and then to the wife of one of Shu's cousins. Her husband was a doctor and the wife thought I was out of my mind."

"For wanting kids with the guy?"

"No, because two years before that—while I was here visiting Eve for a week—Shu had stayed with them in New York after having the vasectomy her husband's partner had done on him, which Shu had told them was a decision we'd made together."

Boone frowned in confusion. "He didn't want kids and rather than let you know, he just went behind your back and got snipped?"

"Oh, it was nowhere near that simple. Although that was basically what he said when I confronted him. But there was something else his cousin's wife had said to me that started me wondering about more than the vasectomy."

"She told you there were freakish genetic mutants hidden in the basement?"

Faith shook her head. "She said she should have known he was doing it behind my back. That not much of anything in that family was the way it looked on the surface."

"So it *was* mutants in the basement?" Boone said as he poured them both more wine.

"No, no mutants in the basement. But Shu did have two beautiful kids on the other side of New Haven."

Boone froze, staring at her a moment in astonishment before he said, "From a first marriage you didn't know about?"

Faith shook her head. "From an ongoing relationship he had with the daughter of his mother's maid."

"How'd you find *that* out?"

"I followed him." Tears stung her eyes and she blinked them back. "Actually, Nedra and I followed him in Nedra's car so he wouldn't spot us. We watched him pull into the driveway of this nice suburban house. A little boy—who I later learned was born the year before I met Shu—came running out to give him a big hug. Behind the little boy came a woman carrying a two-year-old."

Boone flinched. "He had one before he married

you and he'd had the vasectomy after the second kid was born—*while* you were married?"

"He thought two illegitimate kids was his limit."

Boone shook his head in disbelief and the expression on his handsome face was one of confusion. "So he was just keeping this family on the side?"

"The woman was who he loved—it was as simple as that. But there was no *marrying* the maid's daughter—his family wouldn't hear of it, his friends would have turned their backs on him, the woman would never have been accepted, it just wasn't done. Although I learned later that it was pretty widely known among his friends and the rest of his circle that he had this little family, but as long as he kept up appearances, everyone pretended they didn't exist."

"And you were part of the appearances?"

"I was the cover wife, the beard. His parents settled for me even though I wasn't an ideal choice for their son and heir because everyone else in their circle knew the situation and no one was willing to marry him under those conditions. So he went outside the circle, picked someone who didn't know what was going on and could be shaped to fit the mold. Everything I was interested in and wanted in my life—my education, being able to talk about art, music, ballet—all worked to their advantage. Because of it, once they'd *groomed* me I could hold my own with them, I could work on their charities and committees, I could do whatever they needed, go wherever they wanted me to go, talk to anyone there was to talk to, be included the way the maid's daughter never would have been."   .

"While *Shubert* went on having his secret family?"

"Oh, yes. In fact, when I found out and confronted him, he said it was a relief that I finally knew so he didn't have to work at hiding it from me anymore. *I* was really the side dish, not her—she was the main course. They had a life together. Kids. In fact, the vasectomy was a show of loyalty to her—she didn't want him having kids with me. Not even his parents knew about that. They thought I was going to give them grandchildren they could claim."

"Wow," Boone said in amazement.

"And now you know why it was nice to hear that I was your dream girl. Even if it was in high school, it was still a nice ego stroke to find out that I was *somebody's* dream girl since I definitely wasn't that for the man I married," Faith concluded wryly.

Boone's cell phone rang just then. He apologized as he took it out of his pocket and checked the display to see who the call was from. "It's about a sick mare I saw this morning—I need to answer," he said.

"I'll clean up in here—you can have some privacy in the living room if you want it," Faith said, hoping as soon as Boone left the kitchen that this wouldn't put an end to the evening.

Yes, it was getting late. Yes, they had the wedding of her cousin and his sister the next afternoon. And yes, Faith knew it was better if this simple dinner was all they shared tonight.

But none of that changed the fact that she didn't want their time together now to end yet.

Especially when she felt so drained after having told him about her past and knew that if anyone could pick up her spirits again, it was Boone....

"Uh...am I interrupting something?"

Faith shot a glance through her legs at Boone's booted feet and bolted upright so her rear end wasn't the first thing to greet him when he rejoined her in the kitchen. That *hadn't* been her intention.

He'd still been on the phone when she'd finished cleaning their dinner mess. She'd poked her head into the living room and overheard something about fever and vomiting and opted to stay where she was. But after two days of lifting and toting flea market merchandise and display tables, she had a cramp in her back. In an attempt to ease that cramp she'd bent over at the waist and let her arms dangle to the floor. That was the position she was in when Boone found her.

"What are you doing?" he asked when she turned around to face him and found a smile that said he'd enjoyed the view.

"Backache," Faith answered. "I was trying to get the kink out."

"Where does it hurt?"

She told him, pointing as well as she could to the spot beside her spine that was bothering her.

"Come with me," he ordered, motioning with his index finger for effect.

Charlie had curled up in the doorway between the kitchen and living room and was sound asleep. Boone stepped over the snoozing schnauzer and Faith followed suit, going with him into the other room.

He moved the armchair close to the end of the coffee table, leaving a few-inch gap between the two. "Lie facedown with your forehead on the seat and your face in the space."

"A makeshift massage table?" Faith inquired.

"Pretty much."

It didn't look comfortable. But the idea of Boone giving her a massage held massive appeal.

"Are you a part-time masseuse, too?" she asked as she did as he'd instructed.

"No, but I have thumbs."

Faith didn't know what that meant until she was situated. Boone came to stand beside the coffee table and pressed his thumbs on either side of her spine, walking them up and down her spine several times before focusing on the spot she'd pointed out. Then he applied only one thumb there, pushing hard.

"Take deep, slow breaths," he advised.

Faith did that, too. And while this bore no resemblance to the sensual massage she'd thought she might be in line for, with each exhale the pain became less.

"This is actually helping."

"Acupressure. Tell me when it stops hurting completely."

After a few more minutes it did and she let him know.

He stopped the treatment. "Okay, back on your feet."

Faith did that, as well.

Boone took her hands and placed them on the opposite shoulders so her arms formed an X over her chest. Then he went around behind her, wrapped his arms around hers to pull her against him and yanked her backward until her feet were lifted off the floor and her back made a cracking sound.

"Better?"

"What if I said you broke me?" she asked teasingly.

"I'd take you to the emergency room. Did I break you?" There was no worry in his tone.

"No. I think the kink is gone. Maybe you missed your calling and should be working on people instead of animals."

"Maybe," he said, but with so much innuendo in his tone Faith knew he wasn't being serious.

She expected him to let go of her then but he

didn't. He did, however, loosen his grip so that it somehow went from something therapeutic to just having his arms wrapped around her.

Then his face was beside her ear and in a quiet voice he said, "I'm sorry about last night. I know now why I hit a button not being straightforward with you."

"It's okay," she said, thinking much, much more about his arms around her and being tight against him than about the squabble they'd had the previous evening.

Then, still holding her captive, he added, "I think you still might be *my* dream girl, if that helps at all."

She thought that that wasn't any easier for him to admit tonight than telling her about the high school crush had been last night. In fact, she had the impression that the reason he was telling her like this, from behind, where she wasn't looking at him, was because it wasn't easy for him. And though his type had never been her dream man, she wondered why not.

"I like you too much, Boone Pratt," she said just as quietly and almost more to herself than to him.

He kissed the side of her neck. His mouth was soft, his breath warm against her skin, and she felt way too at home in his arms. But she couldn't make herself move. Not to end something that was such sweet, sexy solace.

She did tip her head to provide more access to her

neck, though. And she also slipped her arms from under his to curl them up and grasp his muscular forearms where they were now folded across her breasts.

Breasts that were once again making their own statement with nipples like twin pearls.

Boone kissed her neck a second time. And then kissed her earlobe, tugging at it with his teeth and flicking it with the tip of his tongue.

Then he turned her to face him and found her mouth with his.

Faith's eyes drifted shut, her hands flattened to his pectorals, and she let herself be carried away by another kiss that was more all-consuming than anything her former husband had ever given.

Boone's arms were around her, his hands worked her back in a massage that was more like what she'd expected before—firm and forceful and sensual.

Their mouths were open and seeking, their tongues paired so perfectly that one seemed to always know what the other was going to do. That kiss alone was awakening cravings and desires she'd barely suspected she was capable of.

Her mouth opened even wider, her tongue grew bolder and she couldn't stop her hands from finding their way under Boone's shirt to the smooth, sleek, satin-over-steel of his back.

Then her T-shirt and his were all that was between them.

Boone didn't hesitate to slip his hands under her T-shirt and continued the massage on her bare skin.

But by then it wasn't the bare skin that wanted his attention the most.

The deep breath Faith took nudged him with hardened nipples and he brought one hand around to her breast.

No bra—that suddenly seemed like the best decision she'd ever made. It was just too glorious to feel his big hand encompassing her ripe flesh.

That ever-tenacious nipple poked insistently into his palm as he pressed and kneaded and aroused. Her spine arched, her shoulders went back, pushing her even farther into his grasp.

Boone tore his lips from hers, raised his forearm enough to bring her T-shirt up and expose her for a split second before his mouth replaced his hand.

He drew her into that dark honeyed cavern, deeply drinking her in, putting the talents of his tongue to work on her nipple until Faith was breathless.

Her pulse was pounding, her blood seemed hot in her veins and there was an awakening deeper inside, demanding even more.

The bedroom wasn't far….

But the couch was closer still.

His mouth was driving her out of her mind….

But was it plunging her into more than she was ready for?

Faith moaned, but only part of it was in pleasure. The other part was complaint. Because she didn't know if she *was* ready for this even if her body was crying *ready or not*. And once that morsel of doubt had made itself known, she couldn't ignore it.

"No, we have to stop," she said as if someone else were forcing her to say it.

Boone upped the ante—his tongue circled her nipple, rolled around it, teased it and opened a channel straight to the center of her that made nothing seem as important as taking this all the way.

But what if letting these feelings rule was a mistake…?

"Really, we have to…" she said in an even breathier voice.

He stopped.

Damn him, but he did.

His mouth came away from her breast and returned to hers, kissing her again as he lowered her shirt. Kissing her again with lips parted and seeking, with a tongue she now knew the glories of on her nipple and was willing to sell her soul to feel there again.

But she couldn't. Not even as she was kissing him back with every bit of the same desperation. Not even as her tongue was answering his every move and initiating a few of her own. Not even when his hand found her breast again and her whole body shrieked with a need for this to go much, much further.

Ready or not…

But she shouldn't. She couldn't.…

She had no idea where she found the will, but she finally broke free of that kiss and applied some pressure to his chest, her palms now flat against him.

"I don't know if I'm ready for this," she heard herself say.

He gave one final squeeze of a breast that was calling her a traitor for robbing it of his touch, then he stepped away from her and looked down at her with clear blue eyes that were as smolderingly sexy as any eyes she'd ever seen.

"Okay," he said simply. "I'd better go, then. 'Cause if I stay—" he shook that heart-stoppingly handsome head "—you won't get me out of here till morning."

The urge in her to make him prove that was so enormous Faith didn't know how she resisted it. But she did. Enough to say, "I'll see you tomorrow at the wedding."

Boone nodded, rocked back on the heels of his cowboy boots and pivoted away from her.

He headed for the front door and she trailed behind, crossing her arms over herself to hide nipples that proved she still wanted him so much it hurt.

At the door he turned around to face her again. He jammed his hands into the back pockets of his jeans as if to keep them off of her and leaned forward enough to kiss her again—a sexy, sexy kiss that any bad boy would have been proud of—before he straightened up and left her feeling deprived because it had ended.

Faith peered up at Boone's cocky, crooked smile as he nodded in the direction of her kitchen.

"The guy in those pictures?" he said. "Weak chin. Mine—" he jutted it out for her to see "—so strong I could break bricks with this thing."

Then he stepped onto her porch and closed the door behind him, leaving her laughing at his joke.

Charlie had slept through everything but the door opening and closing. The dog joined Faith just as she spun around and wilted against the oak panel, thinking about Boone's strong chin. His strong shoulders. His strong back. His strong hands...

Oh, how she wanted those strong hands running over every inch of her naked body right at that moment!

So much that it made her wonder how any hometown boy could do to her what Boone had just done.

But no matter how he'd done it, he'd done it so thoroughly that there she was, weak with wanting him to do it again and sure he'd worked some kind of magic on her and on her dog, who was standing beside her, howling pitifully for the man who had just left them both.

Chapter Eight

It was seventy degrees Sunday afternoon, with a cloudless sky overhead and not so much as a breeze to rustle the bride's white veil as she walked down the makeshift aisle in the backyard of her family home.

As Faith sat with her sisters in the second row of white chairs bordering an aisle that led to a latticed arch woven with mauve roses, she thought that even if she had planned the wedding of her cousin Jared to Mara Pratt, she couldn't have done a better job.

Mara was given away by all five of her brothers. The oldest, Cam, escorted Mara. Boone, Scott, Jon and Taylor followed behind them. All the Pratt men resembled each other and there was no shortage of good looks among them, but one glance at Boone and Faith couldn't force her eyes away.

Dressed in an impeccably tailored suit a shade shy of black and a light gray shirt and matching tie, he might have been the most dauntingly handsome man she'd ever seen. Her heart actually seemed to skip a beat at the first sight of him and she was sure that not a single soul who saw him like that could have called him a hayseed. He stood tall and straight and broad shouldered and confident, and he could have easily been transplanted into the swankiest country club party without anyone questioning it.

But Faith reminded herself that she knew the truth. That while she wouldn't call him a hayseed, he was still a Northbridge boy through and through, and as long as she wasn't sure that was what she could be happy with, she needed to be careful about how far she let things go between them. For both their sakes.

It just would have been so much easier if he didn't look like something off the cover of a magazine.

And make her feel the way he did…

The ceremony was short and sweet and when the groom was allowed to kiss the bride everyone applauded them and kept on applauding as they made the return trip up the aisle. Then the guests were directed to a tent on the lawn.

Only the bride and groom formed the receiving line

and the minute Faith had given her congratulations and best wishes to them, Boone was waiting for her.

"Look at you!" he said with a raised eyebrow of appreciation for her silver Chanel dress, matching three-inch heels and the French twist her hair was done up in.

"Me? Look at you!" Faith countered, unable to keep from giving him another, closer once-over that only confirmed he was something to see.

"Sharp, huh?" he said with enough self-deprecation to let her know he didn't take himself too seriously. "I told you we'd all be handsome devils in these suits."

"You were right," she admitted.

They'd never discussed attending the wedding together but from that point on they just seemed to be inseparable. Certainly Boone didn't leave her side. And Faith liked being by his more than she wished she did. But she rationalized not leaving him to mingle or to sit with Eve and Eden by telling herself that he was a good distraction from thinking about her own failed marriage and dashed hopes and dreams.

As the afternoon progressed, Faith did become aware that there was a common thread of conversation going on around them, though. As they drank champagne, ate lobster-stuffed tenderloin, bacon-wrapped scallops and a variety of salads and side dishes, she noticed that his sister Neily—who was the maid of honor—seemed to have disappeared.

"Where did Neily go and why do I keep hearing her name?" Faith finally asked Boone.

"Don't tell me you haven't heard?" Boone answered.

"Haven't heard what?"

"Everything that's going on about that abandoned car near the ice-cream shop and the house on South Street—the things that came up at the town meeting the other night."

Faith wasn't sure how she'd failed to hear anything in Northbridge, but she obviously had. "All I know about either of those things is what was said about them at the meeting that night."

"Your sisters didn't even tell you?"

"I just met up with them here right before the wedding. We didn't really get the chance to chat."

"Well, you have to get yourself back on the small-town grapevine," Boone advised.

"That's what I'm using you for," she joked.

"And I thought it was only my body you were after," he countered with a streak of orneriness that made her laugh and blush at the same time.

"Quit fooling around and tell me what's going on," she commanded.

Boone grinned as if he knew exactly what was on her mind to cause that blush but he didn't say anything about it. Instead, he told her what she wanted to know.

"First up, the cops found out that the abandoned car was registered to the nurse-caregiver of an elderly woman in Missoula who apparently took the nurse's keys during the night and disappeared. There's been a search for the woman and *that's* who they found in the house—"

"Wait a minute," Faith interrupted. "An old woman sick enough to need round-the-clock nursing stole car keys and drove from Missoula to Northbridge by herself?"

"She isn't physically sick. According to whoever Cam talked to about her in Missoula, she has Alzheimer's disease. Anyway, yeah, she drove to Northbridge, left the car at the ice-cream shop and walked to the house on South Street—that's who's been in there."

"Who is she?"

"Her name is Theresa Miles. She actually owns the house."

"Nobody knew that until now?"

"Some of the old-timers did, but the place has been vacant for so long it never occurred to anybody that she might be there. From what I've heard, Theresa Miles moved away when she was seventeen. The local real estate agency has an ancient contract that pays them an annual fee through an estate attorney to go in periodically to make sure the heat is on just enough for the pipes not to freeze and to keep an overall eye on things. But there hasn't been any actual contact about the property in as long as anybody can recall. I don't know how old Theresa Miles is now—all I've heard is *elderly*—but it has to have been a *lo-ong* time since she was seventeen."

"And she has Alzheimer's and still remembered the way back to Northbridge, to her house?"

"I guess that's how it can be with that disease—she couldn't remember her current address or phone number but yeah, she made it here. And had the wherewithal to pry open the padlock on the cellar door and get in that way. But now that she's at the house there's no getting her out of it. Cam and the rest of the police force tried and she barricaded herself in one of the bedrooms upstairs, screaming that she wants what they took from her and that she wasn't keeping quiet anymore."

"She wants what Cam and the police took from her?" Faith asked in confusion.

"No. Nobody knows who *they* are or what was taken from her or if something really *was* taken from her or what she's keeping quiet about or if the whole thing is just a delusion. The family has been contacted and her grandson is on the way, but in the meantime, since Neily is a social worker, she's taken over the case. And because the old lady goes ballistic whenever anyone even mentions her leaving the house, Neily is staying there with her. So that's where Neily is now."

"Neily is staying with a woman who's barricaded herself in a bedroom in a house no one has lived in or taken care of for who knows how long?"

"Neily is good at what she does—she calmed the woman down, promised her that no one would make her leave if she came out of the bedroom and even got her to agree to let Neily stay with her. Neily says the place isn't in all that bad of shape, considering. It needs a good cleaning and some paint and repairs, but otherwise the plumbing still works, the power is on and it isn't so horrible that the two of them can't live there for a couple of days."

"When did all this happen?"

"Last night and this morning. Cam and Neily barely made it to the wedding."

They'd talked through the bride and groom's first dance and the guests were joining the new couple on the floor in the center of the tent for the second song.

Boone glanced in that direction and then stood and held out his hand to Faith. "Now come and dance with me so I can talk you into going to my basketball game tonight after Jared whisks my sister away for her honeymoon."

Faith dragged herself out of her curiosity about all Boone had just said and looked from the dance floor to his outstretched hand.

Then she raised her eyes to his handsome face. "You dance, too?"

He did the cocky smile again. "Try me and see," he challenged.

She took his hand and stood, knowing that whether it was a dance at the wedding or a basketball game tonight, refusing herself his company once she had it was not something she was likely to do.

Faith could not have been less interested in anything to do with any sport. Yet she *did* go to Boone's basketball game Sunday night and enjoy herself.

She also enjoyed herself after the game when she and Boone went to the restaurant and bar on Main Street called Adz. The place was packed with the rest of the team of local men who called themselves the Northbridge Bruisers and got together to play whatever game was in season, and with the large number of townsfolk who turned out to watch them.

There was jovial company and beer and pub food aplenty. But while it was great fun to be a part of the crowd of good-hearted old friends and acquaintances, by late that night Faith was tired of socializing.

With everyone, that is, except Boone, whom she felt she hadn't been completely alone with the entire time they'd been together.

"This has been a full day," she said as she settled into the passenger seat of his vintage sports car.

"Tired?" Boone asked with a glance at her before he pulled away from the curb.

"Just of being around a big group," she confessed.

He gave her a small smile. "Me, too."

Faith angled in her seat and put the side window to use as a headrest so she could look at Boone's profile as he drove.

"What?" he asked about her scrutiny.

Faith smiled the same kind of smile he had a moment before. She was cataloging all the ways she'd seen him today—from dressed in his very fashionable suit, to wearing basketball shorts and T-shirt and back to the jeans and plain blue shirt he had on now. "You've been a man for all seasons today," she said.

"Suit, jock, me," he named them for her. "Let me guess—you liked the suit best."

She was surprised herself to find that not to be true. "You looked fantastic in that suit but you're right, this is you, the jeans."

He took his eyes off the road to glance at her again. "Don't think I didn't notice that you put yours on tonight."

She arched an eyebrow at him. "But the reviews are still out."

He was being jocular because he smiled another, even more enigmatic smile and said, "I haven't been able to get past the sweater."

It was a tight angora turtleneck that left no curve hidden and was aided by the bra she was wearing underneath it that raised, separated and accentuated. And even though she'd been fishing for a compliment on the jeans, it was gratifying to know he'd noticed the top, too.

She'd done all the fishing she was going to do, though, and since he wasn't offering any more on the subject, she changed it.

"I think that between the flea market, the wedding and tonight I've caught up with all there is to catch up on, and it occurred to me a little while ago that I now have the whole scoop on everyone but you."

He cast her another sly smile. "What *whole* scoop?"

"Who married whom, who's divorced, who's engaged, who wants to get married but hasn't found anyone yet, who doesn't ever want to—"

"Ah, *that* whole scoop."

"But not about you," she reiterated. "Is there some secret?"

"Around here? How could that happen?"

"I hadn't heard about the abandoned car and Theresa Miles."

"Yeah, you were *hours* late on that one."

"So are you just the town bachelor or what?" Faith asked.

He laughed. "Like there's only one of us? 'Cause I have to tell you, there are a lot of unmarried guys around here. And women, too, in case you haven't kept score for anybody but me."

"But you haven't ever been married?" she said, cutting to the chase.

"Nope."

"How come?"

He shrugged. "I don't know. It just never got that far with anyone."

"You've never been serious with *anyone?*"

"I've been serious a couple of times. With a couple of different people. Just not serious enough, I guess."

"Anybody I know?" she asked.

"Nope."

"So who were they?"

"The first one was a woman named Sara. We met in vet school and dated all through it. It ended when we graduated."

"Just like that? Spontaneously? You got your diplomas and it was *see you around sometime?*"

Boone looked at her again. "You want the whole story, huh?"

"I didn't give you the Cliff's Notes, I gave you the details," Faith said.

"Okay, fair enough." He didn't sound eager to give his own details but he was conceding. "No, things with Sara didn't just *spontaneously* end when we graduated. But we *were* graduating and we needed to make decisions about where to go from there. That meant where the relationship would go, too. I wanted to come back here to practice, she wanted to go back to her own hometown in Iowa."

"And neither of you was willing to reconsider for the other?"

Boone shrugged. "There was a lot of talking and debating and hashing out. But in the end, no, neither of us was willing to change where we saw ourselves. So she went her way and I went mine."

"Without hard feelings?"

"Without resentment, if that's what you mean by hard feelings. But not without some sadness and remorse and regrets that it hadn't worked out."

Faith could tell by the frown that was wrinkling his brow that he didn't want to go into that part any more than he had. And since he hadn't forced her to dwell too long on the emotional portions of her own past, she didn't push him.

Instead she said, "Who was the second person?"

"Her name was Kathy," Boone said, still sounding not particularly thrilled to be talking about this even as he took a roundabout path to Faith's house. "Kathy was a horse trainer I met in Billings. We did the long-distance thing for about a year, then she moved here—"

"To *live* with you?"

"Yeah," he admitted reluctantly.

"That sounds more serious." And Faith liked it even less. Although she didn't know why it should bother her to think of him seriously enough involved with someone to live with her. "How long were you together?"

"There was the year of dating, and we lived together for not quite two after that."

"But you didn't get married?"

"She wanted to. That was how things ended—she reached the point where it was go on to that or else."

"And you didn't want to go on to that?"

"Don't get me wrong, it isn't that I didn't—or don't—want to get married someday. I do. And I'll admit that Sara and Kathy both seemed perfect for me—I got along with them, we were compatible, we had a lot in common, we liked the same things and they were good people, I can't say anything bad about them—"

"So what was wrong?"

Boone shrugged. "I guess it's a little like what you said last night about your ex—on the surface everything looked great—"

"But they both had hidden families?"

"No," he answered with a slight chuckle. "But that was all there was—the surface stuff that connected us. In the end there wasn't a...spark. It was like...say you have a red wire and you match it up with another red wire and then flip the switch but nothing happens—from the looks of it, it *should* work. But for some reason it just doesn't. Not enough to do the until-death-do-we-part thing, anyway."

"You felt about them the way Shu felt about me instead of the way he felt about the mother of his kids," Faith concluded before she even realized she was going to say it.

Boone took his eyes off the road to look at her, but before he could comment about what had just slipped out, she said, "Was she hurt that you didn't want to marry her—the Kathy person—after changing her life to move to Northbridge and live with you for two years?"

"Some, sure. But the conversation got started by her telling me she'd run into the guy she'd been serious about before me. That she thought she might still have some feelings for him."

"She cheated on you?"

"No, it hadn't gone that far, but she told me he'd talked about working things out with her, trying again. Marriage and having kids was what she wanted and she said it didn't look like we were going in that direction, that if we weren't, she was willing to consider giving the other guy a second chance to have what she wanted."

"And you told her to consider it?"

"Not like that—not offhand without thinking about it."

"But after thinking about it?"

"Like I said, I didn't feel a till-death-do-we-part kind of spark. And if she had I don't think it would have been so easy for her to go back to the other guy—which is what she did. She married him and they have one kid and another on the way."

The trip from Adz had amounted to a zigzagging through most of Northbridge but they eventually arrived at Faith's house.

Boone pulled into the driveway, turned off the engine and angled enough in his seat to face her. "But if you take anything away from this, don't let it be that I felt about Sara and Kathy the way your ex felt about you. Take away that there wasn't anything wrong with you any more than there was anything wrong with them. There's just no accounting for why sparks fly and a real connection gets made between some people and not between others. Yeah, my situations with Sara and Kathy were like yours with *Shubert*— they all had the right stuff when it came to what met the eye, but underneath, where it counts, something was missing."

Faith smiled at how he'd worked that around again to that slip of the tongue she'd made. "So there's a moral to this?"

He answered her smile with one of his own, sending his cheeks into those creases that made him look boyish and charming and sexy all at once. "Seems like there could be," he concluded before he pivoted in the opposite direction, opened his door and got out of the car.

Before he made it all the way around to her side, Faith had gotten out, too.

She was debating about whether or not to ask him in—wanting to and worrying where it would lead if she did. It didn't make that decision any less complicated when they headed for the house and he took her hand.

He kept hold of it as they reached the front door. But as she unlocked it and prepared to step inside, he tightened his grasp of her hand to keep her with him on the porch.

Then he raised it over her head and said, "Let me get a look at the jeans," and turned her around in a circle while he openly ogled her.

"Oh, yeah…" he said in a gravelly voice. "You look as good in those as I thought you would." Then, when she was facing him again he shook his head and added, "But I still just want to get you out of 'em."

Faith couldn't help smiling at that. Or being pleased by it. And not only was it nice to hear she could do justice to the jeans he liked, she was also happy simply to have the pall their conversation had left lifted. Although it did make her even less inclined for this evening to end.

So maybe I should just invite him in….

He lowered their hands, clasping hers to his chest to bring her in close. Then he leaned over and nudged her hair out of the way so he could kiss the side of her neck, sending little bolts of lightning skittering all through her.

"Aren't you coming in?" she heard herself ask, as if she'd assumed all along that he would.

"Nope," he said simply, straightening up to peer down into her eyes. "Not ready means not ready," he said, referring to the reason she'd ended things the night before. "But I can't go through that door and leave it at that, so I'll say good night out here."

Oh.

That was so chivalrous.

And disappointing…

But was she any more ready tonight than she had been last night?

Last night she'd been afraid of making the decision in the heat of the moment. But there wasn't much heat in this moment. Just the undeniable fact that she didn't want him to go. That she wanted him to kiss more than her neck. That she'd spent a nearly sleepless night wishing he were there with her, wishing that she *hadn't* sent him home, wondering what harm would have been done if she hadn't….

"Tonight might be different," she said quietly.

"Yeah?" he said, raising a hopeful eyebrow.

"I was worried before about it being a rash act," she confessed.

"Nothin' rash about this," he allowed.

"No, there isn't," she said. Although even as she did, she knew that she hadn't stopped being stirred up by him in the last twenty-four hours so she wasn't completely clearheaded, either.

But what harm was there in giving in to something she wanted as much as she wanted Boone?

It wasn't as if they were still in high school, as if they were kids. She was a full-grown woman. She was single, free. Certainly he was free and single and a gloriously full-grown man....

"Tonight might be different," she repeated in a breathy voice.

Boone kissed her. A warm, soft kiss filled with promise held in check, as if he were giving her something to think about without trying to cloud things. His sumptuous mouth on hers made it easy to remember what she *had* felt last night. To remember that he'd awakened things in her that her husband never had. Things she could let take over now. Things she could indulge in so she didn't end up the way she had last night—going to bed alone and wanting him almost more than she could bear....

No, she wasn't being carried away now. Terribly, terribly tempted, but not carried away. The choice was hers. Boone was willing to leave her untouched if she still didn't think she was ready.

It was Faith who stopped the kiss so she could say, "Come in."

"On only a tonight *might* be different?" he asked with a patient smile.

She shook her head. "Because it is different."

His smile became a grin and this time when Faith moved toward her front door she used their clasped hands to bring him along.

He closed the door behind them and without the porch light's glow they were in near darkness, the only light inside coming from one she'd left on over the sink in the kitchen.

Faith didn't flip the switch on the wall to provide more illumination and neither did Boone, but Charlie was already there to greet them.

Boone gave the schnauzer a little attention, then told Charlie to go back to her bed in the middle of the sofa. Charlie, as usual, listened to Boone.

"You really are a miracle worker," Faith whispered.

"You ain't seen nothin' yet," he joked as he pulled her around to face him, taking her into his arms to kiss her again.

Only this kiss was not at all like the one on the porch. The one on the porch could have been seen by any passersby and not have scandalized even the churchgoers. But this kiss was a kiss unleashed.

Lips were parted and tongues met and Boone held her so close his left hand had to cup the back of her head to support it against the onslaught. His tongue wasted no time finding hers in a coy game of dodge and dart, lunge and parry, that began to make good on the promise of that chaste porch kiss.

Faith's arms went around him, too, her hands splayed against his broad back. And although she didn't know where it came from, she had the overwhelming sense that it felt right, that she felt right and at home in Boone's arms.

But they didn't need to stay standing at the door. Not tonight.

She drew that kiss to a conclusion, too, taking Boone's hand again to show him the way to her bedroom.

Scant moonlight lit the other room and again Faith didn't add to what was already there. Once more Boone pulled her to him to kiss her with a mouth open wider still and a tongue that knew no timidity. But this time he didn't brace her head; his hands snaked under her sweater to her bare back.

Not only did she revel in the feel of his big hands on her skin, but Faith took it as a suggestion and tugged his shirttails free of his jeans. But she didn't want only to copy him, only to have that limited access to his back—however spectacular it was. So once his shirt was untucked, she found the buttons down the front of it and began to unfasten them until it hung open.

Boone ended that third kiss so that he could pull her sweater off. When he had, Faith shook her head to put some kind of order to her hair again and as she did she caught sight of his naked torso lurking behind that open shirtfront. Carved pectorals narrowed to taut abs.

She slid her hands over his shoulders to sweep the shirt off completely, kissing his chest just once before he took both sides of her face in his hands to bring her mouth back up to his.

Brash and bold and demanding, that fourth kiss was a shamelessly sexy preview of what was to come as Boone's hands went around to her back again, found the hook of her bra and unsnapped it, making quick work of slipping it off her shoulders and tossing it aside.

Audacious nipples met the honed wall of his chest as bare skin pressed bare skin while he did the massage on her back that she was yearning for.

Faith couldn't keep the quiet moan of complaint from rumbling in her throat and she felt him smile even as he went on plundering her mouth. He was teasing her, building her anticipation by denying her what she'd thought he would do as soon as her bra was disposed of.

So you want to play....

She kicked off her shoes, keeping the kiss going even as she dropped two inches lower, finding the button on the waistband of his jeans with her hands and undoing it. Down went his zipper, but very slowly. And when it was completely lowered, rather than reach for that steely part of him that obviously wanted to burst free, she let her hands glide up his sides.

He laughed. A gruff rumble as he took her bottom lip between his teeth and tugged.

But he wasn't going to let her get the best of him. From there—as he tormented her with a mouth that did wild and wicked things to hers—he divested her first of those jeans that had been a gift from him and then of the lacy string bikini panties she had on, leaving her naked but still basically untouched.

Faith caught the tip of his tongue gently between her teeth to toy with it while she slipped her fingers just inside the back of his jeans to his fabulous rear end. But that was all he was getting and she let him know by releasing his tongue to place a chaste kiss on his chin alone.

He laughed again—a husky laugh that she loved the sound of and that made her realize that never, not even once, had making love with her former husband been playful. And that she liked it, even though her body was screaming for more.

And that was when Boone brought a hand around to her breast.

She hadn't meant to groan but she did. An instinctive, breathy sigh as she got at least one of the things she'd been longing for almost every minute since he'd taken his hand off her the night before.

Warm and strong and only slightly roughened by

ranch work, he molded that engorged globe to fit his grasp, letting her nipple curl up into his palm as if it had been carved from it. Kneading, caressing, cupping her, blunt fingertips circling and tugging and flicking her nipple into a granite-hard crest....

Play ended there. Boone took her mouth with his and now his kiss was avid and intent. His free hand went to her backside to pull her lower half up against the hard, burgeoning staff still partially contained in the jeans she'd left on him.

But before she could do anything about those jeans, he let her go—he stopped kissing her, his hand abandoning her breast.

He took something from his front pocket, palmed it, then quickly shed his boots so he could rid himself of the nuisance of what remained of his clothes. Then, finally naked himself, he clasped only her hand again and began to cross the room in the direction of her double bed.

With Boone just ahead of her she savored a sight so magnificent it took her breath away. Broad shoulders dipped into his spine and swept down to where two more dimples at the small of his back heralded a perfect derriere.

Then he turned to face her and gave her the other, even better view of a front side that almost shocked her with the evidence of how much he wanted her.

A single bent knuckle raised her face from her admiration of him, bringing her eyes up to his, to the smile on that handsome face, showing an admiration of his own.

Then he kissed her once more. The slowest, most sensual kiss yet. A kiss that said he was going to make love to her.

He urged her to lie on the bed, then lay on his side next to her, again finding her breasts with his hands, but for only a moment before his mouth left hers to press the lightest of kisses to her nipples. First one, then the other before his mouth opened wide to draw her into that place where even more arousal awaited in the form of that talented tongue.

Faith's shoulders pulled back in response but not even the wonders of his mouth prepared her for that moment when his hand coursed down her stomach and reached between her legs.

She couldn't stop the moan, the arch of her back, at that initial contact and what he was doing to her. He knew exactly the right places, the right amount of pressure, the right combination of soft and hard, of stroking and teasing, of when to slip inside and pull out and forward and back again.

Playtime was definitely over. Faith wanted him, needed him so badly she could hardly keep from telling him. She reached for that long, thick staff she'd only glimpsed before, closing her own hand around him and sliding up and down until she'd worked him into the same frenzy.

After one more intense draw of her breast into his mouth, he released her and reached for what he'd taken from his pocket earlier.

"I *haven't* had a secret vasectomy," he said in a raspy voice as he applied protection.

Then he returned to her, rising up, straddling her, towering above her in all the masculine grandeur that he was.

He dipped to kiss her again as Faith continued to relish that part of him she wanted inside of her, opening her knees as far as his massive thighs would let her.

Keeping her legs bracketed with his, she felt that iron-hard shaft slip between her thighs and glide upward to that gate that seemed not open wide enough for him. Until the very tip found what his fingers had readied and he slid inside of her with an ease she hadn't expected. Any more than she expected him to pulse his hips against the most sensitive spot, hitting it just right and sending her instantly further than she had wanted to go.

But she couldn't help it. Wave after wave washed through her as his tongue thrust in and out of her mouth while the rest of his body stood poised for her pleasure. And as incredible as it was, she was desperately afraid she'd arrived too soon at this moment and ruined everything, that she wasn't any good at it after all....

And yet, somehow, just as that first climax began to recede, Boone caught hold of it and carried it back the way it had come. He stopped kissing her, he reared up enough to reach down and suck her breast into his mouth, and only then did his hips pull back, pull partway out and glide into her again.

Faith's fingers clasped his broad shoulders and she let him teach her how to move, how to meet him, how to pull away a little herself, how to rebuild her own delight and his.

And hers did rebuild even though she hadn't thought she was capable because it never had in the past. Growing faster, stronger, more intense than the first time, the second caught her in a grip of ecstasy like nothing she'd ever known. It held her breathless and frozen in a rapture so sublime it didn't matter that she nearly rose off the mattress with bare breasts blazing, that she cried out, that she called Boone's name.

Boone, whose entire body tensed above her, inside of her, just as she reached the crest and passed over it enough to be aware of him again. Whose arms locked to hold him high with muscles bulging and tendons tight as he drove more completely into her than she'd thought possible, his ruggedly beautiful face giving evidence to a peak more powerful than she'd ever inspired before.

And then with one final, deep, deep embedding into her, he stayed stone-still for a moment before he exhaled and began to relax on top of her.

It took a moment for both of them to catch their breath, for Faith's heart to stop pounding.

When she could, she said, "I thought you wouldn't lead me astray?"

He chuckled, a gravelly rumble beside her ear. "I told you—not *never,*" he said remorselessly.

With their bodies still one, he rolled them to their sides so he could smooth her hair away from her face and peer down into her eyes. "Regrets?"

"No," she said emphatically, unable to put into words what she felt at that moment as joy and elation and satiation all took hold of her.

"Do you have regrets?" she asked then, suddenly afraid that it hadn't been as good for him as it had for her, that *she* hadn't been good enough.

Boone's mouth slid into a slow, replete smile as he shook his head and closed his eyes. "You'll never know how big a no that gets."

And he'd never know what it meant to her to hear that she'd given as much as she'd received.

Then he opened his eyes, stroked her hair and said, "Can I stay the night?"

"Oh, yeah," she said.

He smiled again and she watched as his eyes drifted shut once more.

Her own were too heavy to keep open so she gave up the fight and closed them.

And as exhaustion took her she realized that nothing she had ever experienced before had been as simple or as pure or as perfect as that moment in Boone's arms, falling asleep.

Chapter Nine

"It's a good thing I can nap on the plane today."

It took Boone a moment to figure out what Faith meant—why she'd be on a plane, where she was going.

They were lying in bed at barely 7:00 a.m. on Monday and they'd just made love for the fourth time since leaving Adz after his basketball game Sunday night. He was lying on his back; she was nestled against his side. Her head was on his chest; his arms were around her and he was feeling the effects of having had almost no sleep himself. Maybe that was why he was slow on the uptake.

Then he remembered.

She was going back to Connecticut today for her friend's gallery opening.

His arms tightened around her reflexively. "Sorry, that trip's been canceled. Didn't anybody tell you?"

Faith laughed and her breath was a cotton-soft warmth against his skin. "Why do I think that you're lying just to keep me in this bed so you can have your way with me whenever you want—like you have for the last seven hours?"

"I thought it was you having your way with me," he countered, kissing the top of her head.

"That's your own fault—if you hadn't opened my eyes to how this could really be…"

She let that sentence dangle as she pushed her hips against his thigh. It was enough to make him start thinking about going for number five. Except now he had Connecticut hanging over his head.

"It was pretty damn good," he agreed.

"It was better than that for me," she confessed quietly.

"It was better than that for me, too," he admitted, confused as to why she felt the need to say it.

She tipped her head back to look up at him. "Was it really okay for you?"

She doubted it?

"Are you kidding?" he asked, peering down at her.

"It's not as if I want a rating," she said, but he could tell that for some reason she needed reassurance.

"I just…" she continued haltingly. "The reverend's granddaughter didn't dare do this before she married Shu. He was my first and only. And it was never anything great with him—maybe because he didn't really want to be with me and felt he was cheating on the woman he wanted to be with. But maybe it wasn't anything great because *I* wasn't—"

"Whoa, whoa, whoa—you're afraid you weren't up to snuff?"

She shrugged.

He laughed. "Four times and I'm lying here craving another one for the road. You think that's because it was just so-so?"

"I only know that it wasn't so-so for me."

The awe in her tone made him laugh again. And gave his ego the boost of a lifetime.

He rolled her onto her back, pinning her to the mattress to gaze down into that face that was so exquisitely beautiful even first thing in the morning that he had to stroke her cheek just to convince himself she was real.

"That's it, no Connecticut, no office hours, nothin'. You're stuck here until you're convinced that you knock me for a loop every time."

She smiled that smile he saw in his dreams, apparently relaxing her concerns that she might have come up short somehow, and said, "Connecticut and office hours can't be put off just so we can boink our brains out."

"Boink?" he repeated. "That's what this has been for you when for me it's been waves crashing against sea cliffs, blazing infernos, worlds colliding…."

"I *must* have been good," she joked.

"What do you think?" He was getting hard again and he flexed against her to let her know.

She grinned beatifically. "I guess it wasn't sooo bad for you. But you'd better stop that because we have to get up."

"That's what I'm doing."

"I'm serious," she said with a laugh. "I still have to pack and Eden is coming by to pick up Charlie. And I have to drive all the way to Billings and you have to go to work."

She was right but it didn't stop him from kissing her, his mouth wide open, his tongue flaunting its familiarity. He slipped his hand to a bare breast he never wanted to let go.

But Faith stopped what he probably wouldn't have ended prematurely regardless of what time constraints they were under. "Okay, I believe you—I wasn't awful or boring or mechanical or—"

He kissed her again and proved just how not awful, boring or mechanical he'd found her with another nudge of his hips.

She laid both of her hands to his chest and pushed

until he stopped kissing her once more. "Come on, you know we can't do this."

He did know that. They'd already played around longer than they should have.

He growled a complaint, grumbled, "Yeah, okay," and rolled to his side, freeing her to slide away from him.

"You're sure you don't want to shower here?" she confirmed the conversation they'd had that had led to their making love the fourth time.

"I have to go home and change. Half the people I'm seeing today were with us last night—if I'm in the same clothes it'll take months to stop the gossip."

Faith nodded, pulling the sheet modestly around herself before she reached the edge of the bed where she sat up and put her feet on the floor. "You'd better get going, then."

"I will. I'll dress and take off while you shower."

But even though he should have been in a hurry, he stayed where he was. And so did she.

Boone inched over to her and propped himself high enough on one elbow to kiss the back of her shoulder where it taunted him over the sheet.

"If you stayed we could meet here right after my office closes today and do it all again," he whispered enticingly.

"I can't," she whispered in return.

He swept her hair aside and kissed her nape, flicking the tip of his tongue there to sweeten the deal.

"I can't," she repeated more firmly.

"You could...." he tempted with a nibble on her earlobe.

"Nedra would think I'd been kidnapped and call the FBI. You'd be arrested and put in prison. Animals would suffer, chaos would ensue."

He laughed again and she stood, putting herself out of his reach. But she did turn to face him and even though she had the sheet around her toga-style so he couldn't see the good parts, he got to look up into those violet-blue eyes that could make him melt as quickly as a Popsicle in the sun.

"Go on before you have people waiting for you," she said.

He took a deep, resigned breath and sighed it out. Then he nodded reluctantly, fighting a new urge that took him by surprise—the urge to ask her more seriously not to leave. Not to leave the room, the house, the town, him.

She leaned over and kissed him, a short, sweet, chaste goodbye kiss if ever he'd had one. Then she said, "Charlie will want out the minute she sees you. Would you put her in the backyard for me and I'll let her in after my shower?"

"Sure," he answered, only partially aware of her

request because he was wondering what was going on with him.

Faith had made it to the bathroom during those few seconds he was distracted by his own thoughts, and with the door half-closed, she peeked out at him, smiled and said, "Behave yourself and go to work," before she closed the door completely.

As Boone finally got out of her bed it struck him that neither of them had said anything about seeing each other or calling or having any contact at all while she was gone or once she got back.

So now that their night together was over, that could be it, he thought. There were no plans, no promises, no guarantees that this would go any further.

Which meant that it was possible that he could be relegated to nothing more than any other guy she knew in town.

And even that was only if she really did return from Connecticut…

Boone had only one thing on his mind as he drove home after leaving Faith's house—Faith. She was the only thing on his mind as he fed his dogs and the rest of the animals at his ranch. The only thing on his mind as he hurried through his own shower. Faith and the night they'd just spent together and the time they'd had before that and the fact that she was going to Connecticut.

Connecticut, where there was plenty of all that cultural stuff she loved and couldn't get around here. Where she had friends. Where that weak-chinned guy from the pictures—who was a whole lot more her type than he was—was waiting.

Connecticut, where Faith might decide she'd rather be now, just as she'd decided she wanted to be there eleven years ago.

Connecticut could swallow her up and never spit her out again.

The one night they'd had could be the only one he *ever* had with her....

By the time he'd shaved, combed out his freshly washed hair and gotten dressed so he was presentable on the outside, he was a mess on the inside. His gut was tied up in knots, his pulse was racing and he had the sense that something bad was about to happen.

Logically, it didn't make any sense. But logic wasn't what had hold of him.

So he picked up the phone, called his receptionist and told her he wasn't going to make it to the office on time. He said he had an emergency, to postpone whatever appointments she could and to tell those she couldn't that he'd be there as soon as possible.

Then he got into his truck and headed back to Faith's house.

* * *

"Eden, you're not supposed to be here for an—"

Boone could hear Faith's response to the doorbell he'd just rung as she came to answer it. Then she opened her front door and he watched her stop short when she saw him.

She was dressed in a white terry-cloth bathrobe. Her hair hung damply around her face. And if she'd reached out and touched him at that moment she could have felt how that first glimpse of her raised his temperature, even though she didn't have on any makeup or have her hair done, even though she wasn't wearing any of her fancy clothes.

"Boone," she said in surprise.

"I heard—you thought it was Eden. But it's me."

Lame. He didn't know what he was going to say, but he didn't want it to be lame.

She stepped out of the doorway to let him in without hesitation, which he took as a positive sign, and he went in.

"Shouldn't your office have opened fifteen minutes ago?" she asked as she closed the door. "Did you forget something? Is something wrong?"

She was in her bare feet and he towered above her. So why did he feel so damn vulnerable? But he did. He felt like that chubby, pimply, awkward kid from long ago who had had an overwhelming crush on the unobtainable girl next door....

And that was when it all fell into place for him. When he understood what was behind his drive to come back here. When he knew clearly what had been merely a vaguely understood impulse until that moment.

"My receptionist will handle things at the office. I had to talk to you," he told Faith.

"Okay?" she said, making a question out of the single word. "Is everything all right?"

"I don't know. Maybe. It could be. Better than all right, even."

She'd led the way into the living room where Charlie was sleeping in a patch of sun on the carpet. The schnauzer leaped up the minute she saw him and ran to greet him.

Boone was grateful to have a few moments with the dog to put his thoughts in some kind of order. He picked up Charlie and nuzzled her neck to return her greeting before he settled her under one arm so he could scratch her ear the way she liked.

Faith was waiting expectantly, her curiosity apparent, when he said, "I guess I have some things to say before you leave town."

"Okay?"

Again the sole word questioned him.

"You know that crush I had on you all those years ago? I don't think I ever stopped having it."

She smiled as if that pleased her. "And you came all the way back here now to tell me?"

"That's only the beginning. But the crush *was* the beginning and it just occurred to me that maybe it never went away. Maybe I just buried it, hid it even from myself. That maybe that's why it was so damn hard to tell you about it the other night—more than a decade later—why I had to hedge and act the way I did, why I was afraid of going too far out on a limb with it even after so many years. If I had completely opened the lid on it when I told you about it, I think I would have seen that it was still there, alive and well and getting the same kind of grip on me that it had before, just unconsciously."

Faith's expression was baffled. "But you want to talk about it now?"

"I have to talk about what's come of it now. Before you leave and maybe disappear forever."

"I'm not *disappearing*. I'm just going to Connecticut for a few days."

"But you could go and decide it's where you want to be, that the chinless wonder is someone you should let have a shot at you."

"The chinless wonder?"

"That guy in those pictures your friend sent—the guy she's trying to fix you up with."

"Franklin Hempstead. Poor Franklin," she defended even as she laughed at Boone's nickname for him. "He may be a little chin-challenged, but he's a nice man."

"Yeah, that's what I'm worried about," Boone said under his breath. But rather than continue in that vein he opted to bare his soul to her.

"I think that maybe the fact that my crush on you didn't really die is why things never completely clicked with Kathy or Sara, why there wasn't enough spark. There couldn't be enough spark because they weren't you. And even though it wasn't conscious, that was the problem."

"And you've just had this revelation?" Faith asked.

"I have," he admitted. "Driving home, thinking about you leaving, going where you're goin'—yeah, it all just struck me like a ton of bricks. The crush has probably always been there and now…" He shook his head, having trouble believing what he was feeling. "Now it's become more than that, Faith."

"But, Boone—"

"I know—it's all so quick and you're still foggy after your divorce and don't know exactly what you want or where you want to be—I get that. And I'm not pushing you, no matter how this may seem. It's just that…"

He set Charlie on the floor and went to stand in front of Faith, taking both of her shoulders in his hands.

"We're different—I know that. I know I'm not the type of guy you ever pictured yourself with, that I'm the type of guy you ran like hell to get away from. I know Northbridge is still Northbridge—

hardly a mecca of high culture. But I think we can have something here—you and me, together. I think we've had it since you've been back. And I want more of it. A whole lot more of it."

"What does that mean? You want…a commitment? Right this minute?"

"Yeah, ideally, that's what I want. I want to know you'll stick around. That we can build on what's happened between us now. That you'll be my—"

"Oh, Boone, I can't say that so soon," she said, sounding slightly panicked.

He'd pushed too far. Too hard. Too fast. But he couldn't turn back now.

"I want you, Faith," he said flat out, deciding that if he'd come this far he might as well go the rest of the way. "We've known each other all our lives and even if we've just taken it to another level, the time that you've been in Northbridge again has been enough for me to see the real you. To find out that you aren't any of the lousy things I told myself you were eleven years ago. That you aren't high-and-mighty, nose-in-the-air Faith Perry. That you don't think you're better than anybody. But more than that, what I found out was that you're kind and quiet and unassuming, that you're a little shy, a little wide-eyed, even a little naive. That while you aren't one of the rough-and-tumble, outdoorsy, nature-women I thought should suit me, I like the cream puff in you. That we may not share all our interests but that we mesh just the same. That I have a good time with you. Such a good time that every minute I'm not with you, I want to be."

He paused to take a breath after that barrage, and slowed down. "What I found was that different or not," he continued, "we're great together. That I think we belong together."

He'd said she could be wide-eyed and at that moment that was exactly what she was—wide-eyed, her brows arched, her entire face a reflection of the internal chaos he was causing her.

"I'm not sure what to say to all this," she said. "There's so much and it's soon and—"

"It's okay. No matter what I'd like you to say, I didn't come figuring you'd just leap into my arms."

Although that would have been so much easier on him…

"I just want you to think about it all while you're gone," he added. "I want you to leave here knowing how much I want you. That I believe we can have something together that might not be a night at the opera every night, but that's so damn amazing all on its own that it's worth having. Maybe all that art stuff is still what you can't get enough of, maybe the chinless wonder is the kind of guy you still think is right for you, but even if Northbridge can't offer you what you can get in that other part of the country, even if I'm beer and hot wings instead of champagne and caviar, I think I can make you happy here, Faith."

"In Northbridge...." she said softly, ominously maybe.

"You could still visit Connecticut or New York or wherever," he assured quickly, feeling as if location alone might make him lose her. "You could still visit this Nedra person, and have all of that arty stuff you want. I could even go east with you now and then. You could drag me to every museum and gallery and play and—" he grimaced "—and even the ballet and the opera, if that's what you want."

"But Northbridge is where you're rooted," she said.

"It's where my practice is. It's where my family is. It's where a chunk of your family is. And yeah, it's where I want to live and raise kids and grow old. It's still where I fit in—"

"But do I?" she whispered.

"Sure you do—you're one of our own. There's just a little more to you."

He stalled, hating what he knew he had to add to that. But he did have to.

"I guess the question isn't *do* you fit in, it's do you want to," he said.

"I came here to sort out what kind of life I want from here on. I haven't done that yet. I've been too busy with you," she pointed out.

She was looking up at him from beneath a forlornly wrinkled brow and he could see in her eyes how torn she was. More torn than she'd even been before he'd reminded her that he wasn't willing to leave Northbridge.

But it couldn't be helped.

Only now that he'd said his piece, he knew he had to let her go to make her decision.

It took some willpower to make his hands respond, to release her shoulders, but even then he couldn't do it without sliding them down her arms, without taking her hands in his, without bringing her hands up to press to his chest to pull her nearer.

"Okay, that's it," he said, forcing as much levity into his tone as he could to lighten the mood. "Much as I'd like to tie you to the bed to keep you here, I won't. But I couldn't let you leave without putting in a plug for the home team."

She smiled a little and nodded her head, but she didn't offer more than that. And even though he knew he couldn't expect her to, it clenched his gut all over again that she didn't.

"You'd better get to work," she reminded him quietly.

He nodded. "I'd say have a nice trip but I hope it stinks," he joked.

She smiled a better smile. "Well, I know one thing," she said wryly. "I won't be able to ever look at poor Franklin Hempstead again without thinking of him as the chinless wonder."

Boone grinned back at her. "Good."

Then he gave in to one more impulse and leaned over, kissing her like there was no tomorrow, kissing her until he felt her wilt a little against him, until he knew that he could lead her to her bedroom again and give her one more reason not to go.

But he didn't.

Instead, when he ended the kiss, he peered down into her almost-lilac eyes and said, "And for your information, *that's* how you kiss somebody goodbye— not that little nothing kiss you left me with earlier."

Then he put more of that willpower to work and let go of her completely, turning on his heel and walking out of her house without a backward glance.

Thinking as he went that if what he'd just done hadn't been putting his heart out there, nothing was.

But now that he had, he could only wait for Faith to do with it what she might.

And hope to hell she didn't toss it aside for bigger and better things.

Chapter Ten

Faith was pleased with her friend's gallery opening on Tuesday night in New Haven. It was an elegant affair and after two hours of viewing the paintings and sculptures, of chatting with people she hadn't seen in a while, she took a moment to herself to stand alone and survey the event as a whole.

A long table of catered food was positioned at one end of the main room with four uniformed waiters serving. More waiters and waitresses in identical uniforms moved discreetly through the crowd with trays bearing glasses of bubbling champagne. The collection of eclectic artwork on display against the pristine white walls was noteworthy. The faint classical music being played by the all-strings sextet borrowed from the Yale Symphony Orchestra for the night was soft enough to remain in the background. And the two-hundred-plus guests all dressed impeccably in cocktail attire shared quiet conversation and the occasional ripple of laughter.

It was the stuff of which Faith's young dreams had been made and she was enjoying herself. She was in her element.

Not that that had been true eleven years ago when she was fresh out of Northbridge. But after some working and watching, after some listening and learning and a little tutelage from her former mother-in-law to top it off, she was perfectly comfortable among these people, in this situation. And it gave her a sense of satisfaction.

Appreciating, discussing, understanding art and music, able to participate in urbane conversation—this was where she'd always imagined herself. Where she'd wanted to be.

Not that there was anything wrong with Northbridge. Boone was mistaken about her hating it—she hadn't hated it before and she didn't now. It was just different. Northbridge was earthy and down-home; here things were more refined. Here there was more decorum, more structure, more rules....

More rules and decorum and structure?

That struck her as funny.

Even though she hadn't hated Northbridge, growing up she *had* lived there under her grandfather's reign. And that had meant she'd had an abundance of rules. There had been nothing but structure. Nothing but decorum.

So what had she done, she asked herself, just traded one set of dictates for another?

No matter how hard she tried, she couldn't deny that that was basically what she *had* done.

But even so, she decided she didn't regret it. She was willing to use the right fork, laugh not too big or too loudly, wear what was acceptable for every occasion, behave the way a group like this expected her to behave when it paved a path to the things she loved and enjoyed. It was still better than having to live the life her grandfather had demanded—a life that had required her to follow the rules, live within the structure, and sacrifice those things she loved and enjoyed.

And yet it occurred to her that both her circle in Connecticut and her young life under her grandfather's thumb were extremes, but what she'd happened upon in Northbridge since she'd ventured back was a middle ground between the two. A middle ground she hadn't actually spent time in until now, despite the fact that she'd grown up in Northbridge.

And what she'd found in that middle ground

wasn't so bad. It was a place where a pair of comfortable jeans was acceptable attire most anytime, most anywhere. Where voices were raised but in a good way—to happily greet someone or to cheer for a bunch of local guys playing a game of basketball. Where a fine bottle of wine could be enjoyed without fanfare. Where she'd been grabbed in bear hugs when she'd encountered old friends at the flea market or just around town. It was a place where someone like Boone could drop in unannounced with the makings for a hoagie sandwich.

And that was nice.

"What are you doing standing over here like a wallflower? You look a million miles away," Nedra Carpenter said, interrupting her musings.

"Maybe not a *million*," Faith answered, making a joke rather than tell Nedra she had been thinking about Northbridge.

The other woman was a few inches taller than Faith, extremely thin and wore her golden-blond hair long and straight. Tonight she had on a strapless cherry-red dress that was in striking contrast to her shimmering hair and to the slinky black number Faith was wearing.

"No, really," Nedra said, "what are you doing all alone in a corner?"

"I was just taking in the overview—I'd say you're a hit," Faith proclaimed.

"I wouldn't have it any other way," Nedra responded as if she'd never had a doubt. "Apparently you're a big hit, too," she added.

"I am?" Faith asked in confusion, not understanding what her friend was talking about.

Nedra took a sip of champagne and used her glass as camouflage to nod in the direction of a group of men who looked more like they were discussing business than art. "He can't take his eyes off you," she said in an aside.

"Who?" Faith asked innocently.

"You know who—Franklin," Nedra said.

Franklin Hempstead was one of the men in the group.

"And I won't say *I told you so,*" Nedra said, "but he just asked if I thought I might be able to bring you out to his country place this weekend if he put a little house party together."

"And what did you say?"

"That I'd see what I could do."

"And that's what you're here for now? To see what you can do?"

"Mmm-hmm. It's a beautiful place," Nedra enticed. "Tennis courts. An indoor *and* an outdoor pool. A nine-hole golf course. Stables. The grounds roll down to a big, blue lake where we could do some boating—one of Franklin's hobbies. He has his own private chef. He has an advance copy of a movie that hasn't been released to the public yet and he's talking about previewing it in his theater...."

"Uh-huh," Faith said noncommittally, knowing her friend wasn't finished yet.

"He said it wouldn't be a huge party, just something intimate—maybe twelve or fifteen of us. He wants to keep it small because he would like to spend some concentrated time with you. He actually said that—that he wanted to spend concentrated time with you," Nedra repeated for emphasis. "I'm telling you, you could have this man wrapped around your little finger without trying very hard. He *adores* you."

As if on cue, Franklin Hempstead glanced at Faith and smiled.

It was a pleasant smile—not too big, not too effusive, conveying interest but not much more. A smile within the rules.

Faith answered it with the same kind of smile, knowing exactly how to do it, and wanting to kick herself for not being able to think about anything but the fact that he *did* have a weak, almost nonexistent chin.

"So what do you say?" Nedra asked.

After that subtle meeting of eyes, Franklin Hempstead returned his gaze to the other men he was talking to, leaving no one the wiser.

"I don't know," Faith answered.

"The Fosters would *die* if you ended up with

Franklin Hempstead," Nedra reminded. "And this weekend could be the beginning of that end."

"Or it could just be another weekend," Faith said, knowing she sounded lackadaisical but unable to help it.

"I don't think *any* weekend at Franklin's country house is *just another weekend*. So will you change your plane tickets and stay?" Nedra persisted.

"Let me think about it," Faith said.

"I won't tell him *that*. I'll say you have to see if you can change your travel arrangements. But I don't know what there is to think about," Nedra grumbled as she moved on.

Faith knew what her friend would do now. Nedra would wend her way slowly back to Franklin Hempstead so it didn't seem as if either Nedra or Faith were unduly eager for the weekend he was proposing. But when her friend gave the travel-arrangements excuse she would act as if Faith would like nothing better than to spend the coming weekend at his country estate if at all possible.

But as Faith's gaze again drifted to the man in question, she wasn't so sure about lengthening her trip to include a weekend with him. Particularly when Boone popped into her head at that same moment. Boone and that last brief, impromptu appearance he'd made at her house just before she'd left yesterday.

Neither Boone nor what he'd said had been far from her mind since she'd boarded her plane to New Haven, and now, taking in the sight of Franklin Hempstead, Boone was once more at the forefront of her thoughts, replacing her earlier ones about the hometown he was so attached to.

She couldn't help comparing the two men. Dressed to the nines in an Italian custom-made suit, Franklin Hempstead was attractive—his weak chin notwithstanding. He was suave and sophisticated and the epitome of the cosmopolitan man.

And yet, whether Faith compared him to Boone in the suit Boone had worn to the wedding or to Boone in his usual jeans, Franklin Hempstead couldn't hold a candle to the Montana vet. Not when it came to looks and pure male pulchritude.

Still, Franklin Hempstead *was* nice—she hadn't been lying when she'd told Boone that. And Franklin was interesting, knowledgeable and entertaining…

Well, he'd never made her laugh quite the way Boone had, but Franklin could be amusing. And they'd had several rousing conversations.

Rousing but not arousing…

Of course, she'd been married every other time she'd encountered the man; being aroused by him would have been uncalled for. But now that she was thinking along those lines, she couldn't help comparing him to Boone in that department, too—at least insofar as she was wondering what kind of lover Franklin Hempstead would be.

Would he be like Boone—so passionate he'd leave her nearly comatose with pleasure? Or would he be like Shu—by-the-book, dutiful, mechanical?

Somehow she had trouble imagining making love with Franklin to be anything like it had been with Boone—uninhibited, hot, wild, throw-caution-to-the-wind sex. She could only picture him like Shu. But there was no basis for that except that Franklin Hempstead was more like Shu in general than like Boone.

Franklin Hempstead had a lot going for him, she argued with herself. He could have a lot going for him in the bedroom, too. He could be an even better lover than Boone.

Not likely.

Then Faith reminded herself that Boone was cemented in Northbridge and that while she might have enjoyed the middle ground of her hometown, that didn't necessarily mean she wanted to cement herself there, too. She also reminded herself that Boone didn't have any of the things in common with her that Franklin Hempstead did.

So why didn't that seem as important as she thought it should be? As important as it had always been before?

She wasn't altogether sure. Was it those sparks Boone had talked about? Because there was no denying there were sparks with Boone.

But there might be sparks with Franklin, too, if she just gave him a chance.

Except that with Boone there had been sparks long before they'd ever reached her bedroom. Sparks that had caused her to notice every tiny detail about him—and get turned on by them. Sparks that had caused her to be totally unable to stop thinking about him day and night. Sparks that had caused her to want to be with him every chance she could. Sparks that had caused her to die to have him kiss her, touch her, make love to her....

Standing there, looking at Franklin Hempstead, none of that was happening.

But with Franklin Hempstead—or a man like him—she could have all the culture she craved. She could raise kids in the midst of museums and galleries and theater and ballet. She could have the life she'd believed was for her when she'd been living with Shu.

But if she didn't have the sparks—especially now that she knew what having the sparks was like— would she be happy?

It would have been so much easier if only the man who inspired the sparks were the Franklin Hempstead type. But as she looked across Nedra's gallery at the other man nothing happened for her. No matter how hard she tried. She wasn't thinking about how broad his shoulders were. She wasn't wondering how he looked from behind. She wasn't craving his touch or imagining his lips on hers or what it might feel like to be pulled up against his chest. She just didn't care.

Not the way she'd cared about all of that and more when it came to Boone.

But she'd told him it was too soon to be making a choice like this—or any choice at all—and didn't that still apply? She'd only been divorced since December and she'd just agreed to her sisters' pleas to go to Northbridge for an extended stay in order to sort through things. How wise was it to be already considering a man who had told her he was interested in making a commitment?

A commitment!

Just thinking about that gave her the same reaction it had when she'd asked Boone if that was what he was talking about—she felt panicked, overwhelmed, pressured.

But how could she feel anything else when there were three factions pulling at her—her sisters, Nedra, Boone. Four factions if she counted Franklin Hempstead's bid. What if she made the wrong choice?

She'd fought not to give in to the panic yesterday and she fought it again, taking a few deep breaths to regain some control.

Okay, this wasn't about Eve or Eden or Nedra, she reasoned. It certainly wasn't about Franklin Hempstead. And even though it *was* about Boone, it couldn't be about what *he* wanted. It had to be about what she wanted. What she wanted and where she wanted to be, where she wanted her life to go from here.

So what did she want?

Things had been so clear-cut when she'd left Northbridge eleven years ago. But as she thought it over now the only thing that seemed clearcut was that she wanted more nights with Boone like Sunday night. But did she want the commitment that went along with that? The commitment that would have to be at the expense of all that was spread out before her now.

Accepting Boone and Northbridge wouldn't be *completely* at the expense of all this, she reminded herself, recalling his suggestion that if she made her home in Northbridge with him she could come back to visit Nedra whenever she wanted, whenever she felt the need for a little culture. But still, she wouldn't be living here, she wouldn't be in the center of it.

Only the more she thought about it, the more she realized that she'd had all of this. And she'd been telling Boone the truth when she'd said that as good as it had been, it hadn't *all* been good. But more than the bad that had come with the good, it occurred to her just then that what having all this *hadn't* given her was what she'd found in Northbridge with Boone.

With Boone there hadn't been anything superficial—the way her entire marriage had been. There wasn't any artifice, there weren't any secrets. He'd even made himself walk over hot coals to confess his teenage crush on her.

No, she couldn't picture him sitting through an opera or a ballet, but he was still an educated, intelligent, accomplished man in his own right. And more than that, he was a man who was calm and steady and strong and centered. He was solid. He had substance. He was the gold under the glitter.

Yes, it probably was a little soon after her divorce to be headed where it seemed more and more by the minute that she was headed, but she knew instinctively that this wasn't merely a rebound thing, that she wasn't just drawn to someone who had offered comfort and familiarity at a time when she was in need of that. Boone was so much more and she suddenly knew that to pass on what he was offering for any reason would be the biggest mistake she ever made.

Franklin Hempstead glanced at her again just then.

He smiled again.

And again, Faith smiled back.

She'd be going to the country, she thought, but it wouldn't be to Franklin Hempstead's country house. Not this weekend or any other weekend.

Because as difficult as it was for the starry-eyed girl who had wanted out of Northbridge so badly to believe, she'd made her choice.

And that choice was to embrace the middle ground and go back to her small hometown.

To the last man on earth she would have ever believed could get to her....

Chapter Eleven

It was sunset on Wednesday evening when Faith drove up the private road that led to Boone's ranch. There were no lights on in his house and her spirits took a dive at the thought that he wasn't home, that she was going to have to search for him in town.

But just as she was about to make a U-turn to do that, she caught sight of him in the paddock beside the barn.

She turned off her engine and didn't waste any time getting out of the car.

By then Boone had noticed her arrival and he turned away from the horse he'd been working with and went to the railing that surrounded the paddock. But that was as far as he went. Bracing his forearms on the top bar, raising one booted foot to the bottom bar, he watched her as she crossed the yard to get to him.

Faith didn't blame him for being wary. She knew he was probably worried she was coming to tell him that she'd chosen Connecticut and Franklin Hempstead over Northbridge and him.

"Hey," Boone said in greeting when she was near enough to hear him.

"Hi," Faith responded simply, devouring him with her eyes as if it had been centuries since she'd seen him last.

He'd obviously been working with the horse for a while. His cowboy boots, his jeans, his threadbare white shirt, even his finger-combed hair, were all dusted with dirt. He hadn't shaved since at least that morning because there was the shadow of a beard adding scruffiness to his handsome face. And yet, even looking more grimy than he had when he'd met her at his office to care for Charlie's broken tooth, Faith still didn't have so much as a second thought about being there.

"You're a mess," she told him anyway, hiding just how glad she was to see him in any state.

"Yep," he agreed, not offering more than that.

Faith reached the paddock railing, but she didn't touch anything. She was wearing a shirtwaist dress of beige linen that buttoned from the high, stand-up collar to the hem of the A-line skirt that brushed her calves, and even though Boone's disarray didn't put her off now the way it had that first day, she didn't want to get mussed up herself.

"Thought you were still in New Haven," Boone said then.

She would have been if she hadn't spent a small fortune to change her plane tickets and accepted two layovers in order to get here two days before she'd originally planned. But all she said was, "I came back early."

"Yeah? How come?"

She shrugged and decided to give him a hard time. "I missed my dog."

Boone craned to look behind her. "Then where is she?"

Faith smiled. "Still with Eden," she said as if that didn't give her away.

"And you're here…*missin'* your dog…" he said, calling her bluff.

Another shrug. "Guess I'm a sucker for a strong chin."

He laughed but not too freely, still with some reserve. He did rub his stubbled jawline in response to her strong-chin remark, though, and say, "I've been told I have one of those."

"Guess I've come to the right place, then."

He studied her for a moment and Faith wasn't

sure if all that decorum she'd been practicing for the last eleven years was getting in her way, but she was having trouble bringing herself to tell him what she'd decided in Connecticut the night before.

Apparently he wasn't willing to wait too long because he cocked his head slightly to one side, arched an eyebrow at her and said, "Are you up to no good out here, Faith? Is that why you're havin' trouble gettin' out what you came to say?"

So he *was* worried.

"I'm not sure where to start or what exactly to say," she admitted.

"Did you come to tell me you're packin' up Charlie and goin' back to Connecticut?"

Faith shook her head. "I'm only goin' back to Connecticut to visit now and then," she said, mimicking him.

He gave her a slow, lopsided smile. "Is that so?"

"That's so."

Then he got cockier. "Did you come back here for me?"

"Well, I don't know," she said, giving him the once-over. "Now that I see you like this again…"

He rose up and hopped the fence in one lithe movement, landing in front of her in a cloud of dust.

Faith fanned it away but he ignored her distaste, took both of her arms in his hands and pulled her against him.

"Ick! You smell awful, too," she complained.

He grinned. "We'll just have to fix that, won't we?" he said as if it were a threat.

He gave her a rakish, playful kiss that was nothing like the passionate variety she'd been wanting since she left town, then he clasped her hand to bring her along behind him to the back door of his house.

He didn't say anything, just took her to his bedroom, to the bathroom connected to it, and reached into the shower to turn on the water.

"Shouldn't we talk?" Faith asked, having no doubt she was to be included in his cleanup and intrigued by the prospect in spite of herself.

"I'm too dirty, remember?" he said as he let go of her hand. He yanked his shirttails free of his jeans, popped open the snaps that held the shirt closed and stripped it off.

"And so are you now," he added, nodding at the front of her dress.

As Faith brushed the smudges he'd left on her, he bent over and divested himself of his foot gear. Then he dropped his jeans and Faith's eyes traveled on their own from her soiled clothes to his naked body.

"Yep, that's what I came home for," she said, feasting on the sight of his impressive chest, wide shoulders, well-developed biceps and a lower half that was greeting her all on its own.

Boone made quick work of her dress, sending it floating to the floor around her feet.

"But we really should talk, Boone," she said.

"We really should," he agreed incorrigibly as he unsnapped her bra, slid off her panties and led her into a shower that was just big enough for two.

Warm water rained down on them and that was when he kissed her the way she'd expected him to—with lips parted and sweet, with a sexy tongue that took command.

Somewhere during that kiss he reached for a bar of soap and used it to lather them both—her more slowly, more sensually than himself, running it seductively over her breasts, over the taut crests of her nipples, down her stomach, between her legs—heightening her anticipation with every stroke.

She'd never made love in a shower, never made love standing up, never made love as slippery as they did then. But this was Boone and so once more he showed her how much fun making love could be.

Teaching, guiding, strong enough to hold her up between the shower wall and his burgeoning body, he had her wrap her legs around his hips so he could bring them both to an unprotected, unrivaled peak that left Faith wilted and dependent on his support as the water rinsed them clean and they floated back to earth.

When they'd both caught their breath, Boone

turned off the shower and set her on her feet before he grabbed a towel to wrap around them both at once.

Then, cocooned against him, he gave her one more impassioned kiss before he peered into her eyes and said, "Okay, talk."

Faith laughed and let her forehead fall to his chest. "I'm going back to Connecticut where people are civilized," she pretended to complain again.

"Like hell," he countered.

But he did concede to taking her into the bedroom, to getting them both settled comfortably on the bed with Faith lying on her back and Boone on his side next to her, his head propped on one hand to look down into her face as he covered them both with a quilt.

Then he repeated, "Okay, talk."

"No, you talk," she said, feeling suddenly tentative about baring her soul. "Tell me what kind of commitment you were hinting at Monday morning because I have a terrible crush on you and I want to know exactly what you meant before I go *too* far out on a limb myself," she hedged, saying the same things to him that he'd said to her over the course of their last meeting.

"Are you tryin' to finagle a proposal out of me, Perry?" he asked through narrowed eyes.

"I am not a finagler," she said, putting on airs.

"Too bad. 'Cause that's how I'm tellin' it to our

kids and our grandkids and our great-grandkids—
I'm sayin' you went off for a few days to see some
chinless guy who wanted you...."

Boone paused, then he said more seriously, "The
chinless wonder *did* want you, didn't he?"

"He sent messages along those lines."

"But you wanted me," Boone continued, picking
up the cockiness where he'd left off. "So you high-
tailed it home and *begged* me to marry you—that'll
be my story."

"If I *did* beg you to marry me would it make up
for hurting your feelings in high school?"

"It's a start," he pretended injury. "But you have
a ways to go yet."

"Uh-huh. And just how much will it take, do you
think?" she asked, playing along.

"The rest of your life."

"Wow. Those were some really hurt feelings,"
she marveled.

"Yep. Now start beggin'."

"Where *I* come from, the man does the proposing," she said loftily again.

He grinned. "You come from just down the road,
Miss High-and-Mighty."

"Where the man still does the proposing."

He gave her a mock frown. "How do I know you
aren't just settin' me up so you can say no?"

"Maybe because while I was in Connecticut I

realized that when it came to those sparks you were talking about, nothing—and no one—could light them in me the way you do. Maybe because I realized that Northbridge really does have its own appeal and that going back to Connecticut for visits will be enough… Well, it will be if you keep me busy here the rest of the time—say with a wedding and running a household of my own and having kids.…" Faith smiled and finished with a seriousness of her own, "And maybe you can know that I'm not just *settin'* you up so I can say no because I have more than a crush on you, too."

"Is that so?" he repeated.

"That's so."

"You love me?" he challenged smugly.

"With all my heart."

His grin was slow and satisfied and there wasn't a single note of joking in his voice when he said, "Good, because I'm crazy in love with you, too."

He swept in and kissed her again, a long, lingering kiss.

But before things went too far, Boone ended it, looked down into her eyes with his mountain-lake-blue ones and said, "You gonna marry me, Faith?"

"Why, yes, I am," she said without any hesitation.

"And make all my young dreams come true?"

"To the best of my ability."

"I'll see if I can't make a few of yours come true,

too," he promised, kissing her again before he added, "But seein' as how I haven't slept in days, I'm gonna need a little snooze-time and maybe even a shave before I can take another stab at that."

He tucked her more firmly against the front of him, and laid his head on an arm that curved over the top of her head.

Faith could feel the warmth of his breath in her hair, the heat and power of his body sheltering her, and she closed her eyes, too, feeling as if she really had come home.

To this man who was nothing at all like what she'd ever envisioned for herself.

Boone Pratt and Northbridge...

No, neither of those things were what she'd fantasized about.

And yet here she was and here she would stay.

For a moment it hardly seemed possible that she could have ended up like this.

But then she opened her eyes and tilted her head enough to peer at Boone's bewhiskered face.

And she knew all over again that ending up anywhere on earth with this man was the best thing that could have ever happened to her.

And she was just grateful that it had.

* * * * *

*Be sure to look for more of
Victoria Pade's Northbridge Nuptials stories
later in 2008,
only from Silhouette Special Edition!*

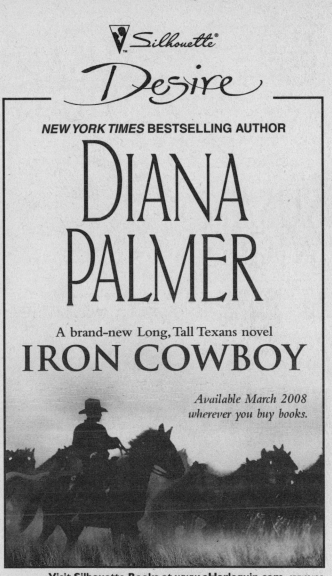

Silhouette®

Desire

NEW YORK TIMES BESTSELLING AUTHOR

DIANA PALMER

A brand-new Long, Tall Texans novel

IRON COWBOY

*Available March 2008
wherever you buy books.*

$1.⁰⁰ OFF

The bestselling Lakeshore Chronicles continue with *Snowfall at Willow Lake*, a story of what comes after a woman survives an unspeakable horror and finds her way home, to healing and redemption and a new chance at happiness.

NEW YORK TIMES BESTSELLING AUTHOR

SUSAN WIGGS

"Susan Wiggs's novels are beautiful, tender and wise."
—Luanne Rice

Snowfall at Willow Lake
The Lakeshore Chronicles

On sale February 2008!

SAVE $1.⁰⁰ off the purchase price of
SNOWFALL AT WILLOW LAKE
by Susan Wiggs.

Offer valid from February 1, 2008, to April 30, 2008.
Redeemable at participating retail outlets. Limit one coupon per purchase.

52608168

5 65373 00076 2   (8100) 0 11463

Canadian Retailers: Harlequin Enterprises Limited will pay the face value of this coupon plus 10.25¢ if submitted by customer for this product only. Any other use constitutes fraud. Coupon is nonassignable. Void if taxed, prohibited or restricted by law. Consumer must pay any government taxes. Void if copied. Nielsen Clearing House ("NCH") customers submit coupons and proof of sales to Harlequin Enterprises Limited, P.O. Box 3000, Saint John, N.B. E2L 4L3, Canada. Non-NCH retailer—for reimbursement submit coupons and proof of sales directly to Harlequin Enterprises Limited, Retail Marketing Department, 225 Duncan Mill Rd., Don Mills, Ontario M3B 3K9, Canada.

U.S. Retailers: Harlequin Enterprises Limited will pay the face value of this coupon plus 8¢ if submitted by customer for this product only. Any other use constitutes fraud. Coupon is nonassignable. Void if taxed, prohibited or restricted by law. Consumer must pay any government taxes. Void if copied. For reimbursement submit coupons and proof of sales directly to Harlequin Enterprises Limited, P.O. Box 880478, El Paso, TX 88588-0478, U.S.A. Cash value 1/100 cents.

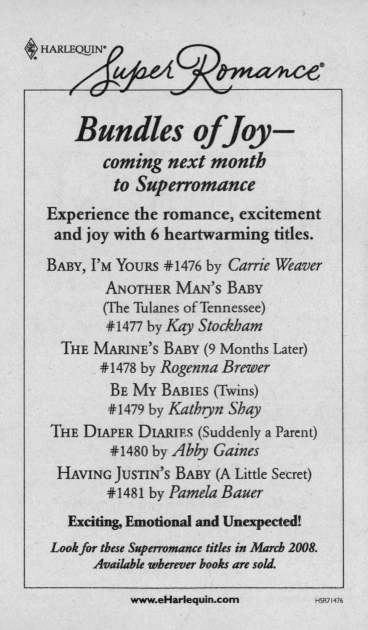

HARLEQUIN
Super Romance

Bundles of Joy—
coming next month
to Superromance

**Experience the romance, excitement
and joy with 6 heartwarming titles.**

BABY, I'M YOURS #1476 by *Carrie Weaver*

ANOTHER MAN'S BABY
(The Tulanes of Tennessee)
#1477 by *Kay Stockham*

THE MARINE'S BABY (9 Months Later)
#1478 by *Rogenna Brewer*

BE MY BABIES (Twins)
#1479 by *Kathryn Shay*

THE DIAPER DIARIES (Suddenly a Parent)
#1480 by *Abby Gaines*

HAVING JUSTIN'S BABY (A Little Secret)
#1481 by *Pamela Bauer*

Exciting, Emotional and Unexpected!

*Look for these Superromance titles in March 2008.
Available wherever books are sold.*

In the first of this emotional Mediterranean Dads duet,
nanny Julie is whisked away to a palatial Italian villa,
but she feels completely out of place in Massimo's
glamorous world. Her biggest challenge, though, is
ignoring her attraction to the brooding tycoon.

Look for

The Italian Tycoon
and the Nanny
by **Rebecca Winters**

in **March** *wherever you buy books.*

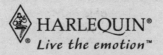

Silhouette®

COMING NEXT MONTH

SPECIAL EDITION

#1885 THE SHEIK AND THE PREGNANT BRIDE—
Susan Mallery
Desert Rogues
When mechanic Maggie Collins was dispatched to Prince Qadir's desert home to restore his Rolls-Royce, she quickly discovered his love life could use a tune-up, too. Qadir was more than game, but would Maggie's pregnancy shocker stall the prince's engines?

#1886 PAGING DR. DADDY—Teresa Southwick
The Wilder Family
Plastic surgeon to the stars David Wilder, back in Walnut River and the hospital his father once ran, was on a mission of mercy—to perform reconstructive surgery on a little girl badly injured in an auto accident. Would Courtney Albright, the child's resilient, irresistible mother, cause him to give up his L.A. ways for hometown love?

#1887 MOMMY AND THE MILLIONAIRE—Crystal Green
The Suds Club
Unwed and pregnant, Naomi Shannon left her small town for suburban San Francisco, where she made fast friends at the local Laundromat. Sharing her ups and downs and watching the soaps with the Suds Club regulars was a relaxing treat…until gazillionaire David Chandler came along, and Naomi's life took a soap opera turn of its own!

#1888 ROMANCING THE COWBOY—Judy Duarte
The Texas Homecoming
Someone was stealing from Granny, ranch owner Jared Clayton's adoptive mother. So naturally, he gave Granny's new bookkeeper, Sabrina Gonzalez, a real earful. But forget the missing money—a closer accounting of the situation showed that Jared had better watch out before Sabrina stole his heart!

#1889 DAD IN DISGUISE—Kate Little
Baby Daze
When wealthy architect Jack Sawyer tried to cancel a sperm donation, he discovered his baby had already been born to single mother Rachel Reilly. So Jack went undercover as a handyman at her house to spy. Jack fell for the boy...and for Rachel—hard. But when the dad took off his disguise, all hell broke loose.…

#1890 HIS MIRACLE BABY—Karen Sandler
To honor his deceased wife's wishes, sporting goods mogul Logan Rafferty needed a surrogate mother for their embryos. Her confidante Shani Jacoby would be perfect—but she was his sworn enemy. Still loyal to her best friend, though, Shani chose to carry Logan's miracle baby…and soon an even bigger miracle—of love—was on their horizon.

SSECNM0208